Bill Freeman

Danger on the Tracks

James Lorimer & Company, Publishers
Toronto, 1989

ISBN 0-88862-872-2 paper
ISBN 0-88862-873-0 cloth

Cover design: Don Fernley
Cover illustration: ONI
Map: Dave Hunter

Photo credits: Regional Collection, D.B. Weldon Library, University of Western Ontario: 1, 7, 9, 10, 12, 16, 18-20. Public Archives Canada: 2(C53563), 4-6(C35489, C46486, PA29542), 14(PA43091). London Historical Museums: 3, 11, 13, 21. London Room, London Public Library: 8, 15, 17.

Canadian Cataloguing in Publication Data

Freeman, Bill, 1938-
Danger on the Tracks

(Adventures in Canadian history)
ISBN 0-88862-873-0 (bound) ISBN 0-88862-872-2 (pbk.)

I. Title. II. Series: Freeman, Bill, 1938-
Adventures in Canadian history.

PS8561.R378D35 1987 jC813'.54 C87-093483-X
PZ7.F73Da 1987

James Lorimer & Company, Publishers
Egerton Ryerson Memorial Building
35 Britain Street
Toronto, Ontario, M5A 1R7

Printed and bound in Canada

6   5   4   3   2   1   87   88   89   90   91   92

The coming of the railroads brought revolutionary changes to Canada. Prior to their arrival, land travel was dependent on wagons and stagecoaches. Poor roads made transportation difficult and incredibly slow. For many people in the nineteenth century the trails of smoke from locomotives streaking across the sky were symbols of progress. Railroads meant that the isolation of small communities was broken and the frontier stage of development was drawing to a close. Not all people, however, welcomed these events.

Danger on the Tracks is a work of fiction, but it is based on the lives of the railroaders and the rural people of Ontario. It describes a part of the real history of the people of Canada.

Bill Freeman

CHAPTER 1

"GET ready!" the girl whispered, crouching by the open doorway of the empty boxcar.

The cool early-morning air blew into their faces as Meg and Jamie Bains leaned out of the train. The locomotive up ahead was wheezing and snorting as it slowed to come into the big railway yards in the east end of London, Ontario. Suddenly there was a long blast of the engine's whistle, and then the squealing shriek as the brakes took hold and the steel wheels began to skid on the rails.

Jamie held onto his sister's shoulder as he leaned out the doorway of the boxcar. His clothes were filthy. Dirty finger marks were on his cheek.

"We've got to jump!" Meg said over the clatter of the wheels. She brushed strands of blond hair from her face. Her hands were smudged with grime from days of hard travelling, and her long dress was dusty. "They say there's railway police everywhere in this yard."

The engine bell was ringing loudly. Overhead they caught a glimpse of the brakeman running along the top of the boxcars. As the train came into the huge yard, Jamie and Meg could see a half-dozen engines shunting cars on the sidings. Men were unloading cargo into wagons.

Meg crouched even lower as the train slowed. She hitched up the canvas bag that was slung over her shoulders. "Now!" she hissed.

She leapt from the moving train, hit the gravel hard and rolled completely over. When she looked back, her brother was still in the boxcar. "Jump, Jamie!"

The boy was frightened. They were going too fast. "Jump!!" Meg called again. He sucked in his breath and leapt into the air. As he landed, his feet were swept out from under him, and he fell heavily on his side.

"Are you all right?" Meg shouted, running up to him.

It was a moment before the boy struggled to his feet. "Think so."

"Come on before they catch us!"

They ran with their sacks bouncing on their shoulders, and only slowed when they got to the street that skirted the north side of the tracks. For a moment they paused to catch their breath, and then began to walk west towards the centre of town.

"I don't know why we're getting off here, anyway," Jamie muttered as he struggled to keep up.

"How many times do I have to tell you? We've got to get jobs."

"That's what you've been saying ever since we left Toronto, but there's no work anywhere."

"The railway's advertising for labourers. You saw that in the newspaper yourself."

"But we're just kids. They're not going to hire us."

Meg looked cross but kept walking. Deep down she knew Jamie was right, but she couldn't admit it. They had been looking for work for days now. Hamilton, Brantford, Simcoe, Woodstock — they had searched everywhere. Restaurants, warehouses, factories, farms — no one had offered them as much as a day's labour.

It was the fall of 1875, and the Depression had thrown grown men out of work. How could a fourteen-year-old girl and a slight boy of twelve ever be able to find jobs? But if they didn't get work soon, they would starve.

Jamie kicked at a stone. "I want to go back to Ottawa."

"Come on, Jamie, you know perfectly well we can't do that. Mother isn't even able to support the other children let alone us."

"If we could only get a solid meal. Then I might feel better."

On the north side of the street neat workers' cottages built of red and yellow brick lined the roadway. As Meg walked past she noticed a boy staring out one of the windows. He reminded her of Robbie, her young brother. She looked enviously at the tiny houses, surrounded by small lawns and gardens. Would her family ever have their own house again?

Absently Meg fingered the worn letter in the big pocket of her dress. It had arrived from their mother the day before they had left Toronto, and the news was not good. She had read the letter so many times that she had much of it memorized. One paragraph worried her most of all.

> Things have not been too good for us in Ottawa. The man who owns the mortgage on our house has taken us to court because we have not been able to keep up the payments, and all our savings are gone. But

I hope to get work soon, so don't worry. Kate is old enough to take care of Robbie and the house. They both miss you a lot.

Meg bit her lip. Ever since their father had been killed in a lumber camp a couple of years earlier, the family had seen hard times, but nothing as bad as this . Meg and Jamie hadn't been able to send the family money since they had left Toronto, and she knew that unless they found work soon, terrible things could happen. Winter was coming. Would Kate and Robbie have enough to eat? What would they do if Mother lost the house? Maybe they would be forced into the poorhouse where they would have to live in one room with a dozen other families.

Meg brushed a tear from her eyes and squared her shoulders. She hurried along the street while Jamie lagged behind. The advertisement she had clipped out of the *Free Press* had said that the London, Huron and Bruce Railway would be hiring that very day.

"That must be the station," Meg said, pointing to a building a couple of blocks ahead. "Come on. It can't be more than eight o'clock. If we're the first ones there we might have a chance."

Jamie hurried faster, taking as big strides as he could and occasionally breaking into a run for a few paces to keep up with his sister. As they came up to the station, a passenger express train waited at the platform. The huge locomotive hissed plumes of white steam from her big boiler and sent up thick black smoke from her bulbous stack. A bell was rung by the stationmaster. The blue-coated conductor shouted, "All aboard!" and was answered by a long blast of the engine's whistle.

Jamie and Meg scrambled up onto the platform to watch. There was another blast, and then the pistons of the engine began to thrust the big driving wheels. The train shuddered as the couplings jarred, and then began to roll slowly forward. With a tremendous *Chug ... Chug ... Chug ...* of the engine, the train began to gather speed and head out of the station for points west.

"Look at that!" said Jamie excitedly. "If only I could get a job working on steam engines." The boy glanced around but found that his sister had disappeared. It took him a moment to spot her talking to the stationmaster.

"They're around the other side of the building at the office," Jamie heard the man say with an English accent. "But I doubt if the likes of you ... "

"Thank you, sir," Meg replied quickly. Then she hurried off down the platform with Jamie close behind.

When she rounded the corner of the station, Meg's heart sank. A crowd of about thirty men, most in their twenties and thirties, hovered around a door. They were working men, rough and ready navvies who looked as if they could do any type of construction work.

For a long moment Meg stood, immobile, wondering what to do. They had travelled a long way on the hope given by the tattered advertisement that she clutched in her pocket. But what chance would a young boy and girl have of getting a job when men like this were available?

Meg was not the type to give up easily. Casually she swung the canvas bag off her shoulder, walked over to a hitching post and leaned up against it. Jamie dropped his bag to the ground and slouched up against the rail between her and a heavy-set labourer.

The man pushed his hat to the back of his head. "What you doin' here, boy?"

"We're looking for work,"

"Work?" The man stroked his stubbled beard. "You an' that girl gonna be labourers?" A smile spread on his face.

Jamie glanced around at the others nervously.

"Maybe you should ask to be a steel-drivin' man, there, boy. They could use a real railroader like yourself." The other men joined in the laughter.

Jamie felt his face burn, but then he noticed Meg standing with her arms folded and a steely look on her face. Slowly he folded his arms and turned away.

A moment later the door of the office opened, and three men came out. One was a big, round-faced man dressed in long striped engineer's overalls and with a black shiny bowler hat pushed to the back of his head. Another was a slight man in a conductor's uniform, with a handlebar moustache and a gold watch chain looped through the buttons of his waistcoat. The third man carried a sheaf of papers. He wore a practical brown suit and fedora.

The crowd of labourers stopped talking and pressed forward. They were a scruffy-looking crew. Many looked as if they had ridden the rails a long way to have a chance at these jobs.

"All right. Get some order there, now," the brown-suited man shouted with authority. "I've got ten jobs here, and I need ten men who'll put in a good day's work."

Meg and Jamie were swamped by the big men pushing ahead to get attention.

"I'll take you ... you ... and that man with the red neckerchief there."

Meg could hear the man talking, but she couldn't even see him in the press of workers. A sense of panic gripped her. They just had to get jobs.

The men pushed forward dangerously. "Me, sir. Over here," one shouted out. "Take me!" called another.

"Settle down there!" shouted the engineer. "There'll be order here or there'll be work for none of you!"

"That's Sam Bolt," Jamie heard one of the labourers whisper.

The boss spoke over the noise. "You men I've hired go and stand over against the wall so we can see who's left." There was a shuffling about, and then the hiring began again. "I'll take you ... and that big-shouldered man there ... "

As the gang was made up, the hired men went, one at a time, to stand by the station wall. Gradually the crowd thinned, and Meg and Jamie pressed to the front of the semi-circle of men that were left. Most of the jobs were taken. Meg knew they had to be hired now or lose their chance.

The boss seemed to be examining each man that was left. "How many more do we need, Sam?" he asked.

"Three more," replied the engineer.

"I'll take you ... "

"Please, sir!" Meg called out suddenly. "Please hire me and my brother!"

"You're just a child. And a girl to boot."

"We'll do anything."

"Give 'em a job carryin' steel rails," called one of the men who had been hired. Others laughed.

Meg didn't care what they thought. "Isn't there something we can do? We've got to have work."

"I'm looking for construction men. This is no camp for girls. We're building a railroad."

"But we can work hard!" Meg pleaded. "We've worked in lumber camps and in a factory in Montreal. We can ... "

The man interrupted her. "I'll take you two." He pointed to a couple of rough-looking characters. "That's all the work we've got."

A feeling of desolation swept over Meg. Their money was almost gone. They were tired and dirty from travelling in boxcars and sleeping outdoors. Maybe they would never find work.

As they turned to go, they could hear the engineer issuing orders to the men who had been hired. Slowly Meg walked down a set of stairs that led off the platform and sat on the bottom step. Jamie sank down wordlessly beside her.

Meg glanced at her brother. In that moment he locked like a little boy who needed a hot meal, a bath and a good night's sleep tucked up in a warm bed. She was supposed to be looking after him but how could she do that when they had no money and no work?

Suddenly there was a commotion out on the street. A stagecoach wheeled dangerously onto the lot where wagons and carriages were parked. It bumped over the ruts, and then the rig was brought to a violent halt in the middle of the yard.

Two men leapt to the ground and strode towards the station. Both were powerful looking, with wide shoulders and narrow waists. The driver was a handsome man in his early thirties. Dark curly hair flowed out from under his broad hat. He wore coachman's boots that came almost up to his knees, and he carried a long horse whip in his gloved hand. The other man, maybe ten years younger, was dressed like a worker in heavy denim pants and linen shirt.

The stage driver paused with his hands on his hips and looked directly at Jamie and Meg sitting on the steps. "Either of you two know the engineer called Sam Bolt?"

"Sam Bolt?" repeated Jamie.

"The one who drives on the steel rails to Huron County and the north of here." He spoke with a soft country accent, but there was anger in his voice.

Jamie got to his feet and looked back at the group of men gathered around the station. "I ... I think he's the engineer there. The one with the bowler hat."

The man slung his whip over his shoulder and sprang up the stairs two at a time. "Bolt ... Sam Bolt! I want to have a word with you." The stagecoach driver stood at the top of the stairs, his feet planted apart. His companion came to stand beside him.

The engine driver turned around, his red face showing surprise. "What is it?"

"These kids tell me you're the engineer who drives the London, Huron, Bruce Line."

"What's it to you?" The two big men confronted each other warily.

"I'm Will Ryan, and this is my brother Bobby. We want to know why it is that you and that train of yours think you've got the right to frighten half the countryside!"

"I don't frighten nobody."

"Ever since that rail line was finished up to Exeter, you've been rushin' back an' forth like an old cock rooster out to prove you can rule the hen house."

Other men began to gather around as they sensed trouble. The shoulders of the engineer tensed. Ryan played with his horse whip and glared out of dark eyes.

"Yesterday, up by Clandeboye, I was drivin' my stage along the London-Goderich Road when you blew that steam whistle of yours. Near drove my horses crazy. Did it on purpose, far as I can tell. Waited for just the right moment and then all hell was let loose with a blast. 'Twas all I could do to hold the team from runnin' into the ditch."

"I've got to blow the whistle for safety."

"Did it on purpose!" Ryan's voice was controlled fury. "Railroads are tryin' to drive the stages out of business."

"Company rules say I have to blow the whistle at all road crossings."

"You'd like to blow every stage off the road, Bolt, so the railroads can take over all of the trade!" Now her was shouting.

"Well, you're going to have to put up with it, Ryan, 'cause the railroad's here to stay. Dobbin's day is finished and the sooner the better. This is the age of the iron horse."

"That's all you know," said Bobby threateningly.

"The stage is the best transportation there is," added his brother. "It's the way this country was built!"

"Locomotives travellin' the steel highway can haul fifty times the load of a stagecoach and get there twice as fast."

"I can beat your rust bucket any day of the year, and I'm willin' to wager fifty dollars on it!"

Sam's laugh was full of contempt. "You'd lose your fifty dollars and prove yourself a fool!"

"Fifty dollars! Are you man enough to match it?"

"It'll be like stealing from a baby."

"Then the race is on?" Ryan was smiling.

"There'll be no races with company property." The man in the business suit who had been doing the hiring broke in with cool authority.

"Who are you?" asked Will.

"George Mason's the name, and I'm the superintendent of construction on that railroad. There'll be no races. I'll not have company property endangered. Is that understood, Sam?"

"Yes, sir," the engineer said without enthusiasm.

"I'll ask you to clear out, Mr. Ryan, and take your stagecoach with you. We've got business to do here."

"Cowards!" muttered Bobby.

Will Ryan stood for a moment, his face frozen. Then his eyes narrowed, and he clutched his whip with a fist. When he spoke, his voice was a growl. "I've asked for a simple wager, and you treat me like scum."

"You'll regret this day," added Bobby.

The driver turned on his heel, and his big boots pounded on the wooden platform. His brother followed. They jumped to the ground, strode across the yard and leapt up to the box of the stage. The horses moved skittishly.

Jamie watched, fascinated. It would take strength and nerve to handle a high-spirited team like that.

Grasping the reins in his left hand, Will Ryan jerked them hard. Then, in one easy, fluid movement, he cracked the whip over the backs of the two horses. In a moment the coach had wheeled out onto the street and was gone.

CHAPTER 2

"IF that don't beat everythin'?" Sam Bolt muttered under his breath.

"Who are they?" asked Jamie.

"The Ryan brothers. Four of them run the stage line between here and Exeter. This country's filled with hotheads like that."

"Seems like he could cause real trouble."

"Full of bluff and vinegar. That's all." The engineer took a big red handkerchief out of his pocket and mopped his brow. He looked at the boy with curiosity. "They seemed to know you."

"He came up and asked for Sam Bolt. I just pointed you out to him."

"Mmmm ... what are you two doin' here, anyway?"

"Looking for work, sir," said Meg. "We've been travelling all over but can't find anything."

"Where's your parents?"

"Our father's dead. We've got a brother in Newfoundland. Mother and the rest of the family are in Ottawa."

"Lost waifs out tryin' to support yourself. There's thousands of others like you ridin' the rails. You've got nothin' but starvation ahead."

"Do you think ..." Meg paused. "Do you think you could help us find a job, Mr. Bolt ... sir?"

The red-faced man wiped his face again, studied the girl and then looked back at Jamie. "We're a railway, not a charity."

"Yes, sir. I understand." Meg glanced at her brother and then looked down at the ground. Without speaking, the two young people went to sit on the steps again while the engineer rejoined the other railroaders.

A couple of moments later Sam called to them. "Hey, you two, come here."

They scrambled to their feet. The engineer was standing beside George Mason, studying them carefully. Meg nervously straightened her dress and tried to tuck her hair into her bun.

The railway supervisor pulled a freshly lit cigar out of his mouth. "Sam tells me you are desperate for a job."

"We rode freight trains all the way here because of that advertisement you put in the papers," Meg said timidly. "We have no money left."

"Are you willin' to put in some hard work?"

"Yes, sir." Meg nodded anxiously.

The supervisor puffed on his cigar while he regarded them. "I've a railway to build. I don't run an orphanage. Everyone here has to pull their own weight."

"We've always worked hard, sir."

"All right, then. I'll give both of you jobs helping the cook in the construction camp at the head of the steel."

"Mr. Henry's not gonna be happy," said the conductor. "Young kids and all."

"He'll just have to put up with it," said the superintendent, looking back at the young people. "Thirty-five cents a day each you'll be paid, and I promise you this. The railroad's the school of hard knocks. You'll put some sweat on your brow, or you'll be out riding the freights again. Understand?"

Meg was beaming. "Oh, yes, sir!"

"Get yourselves washed up, then. The pair of you look a right sorry mess. Sam, here, is takin' a trainload of men and supplies up to the camp this afternoon. Make sure you're on it."

Meg was nodding enthusiastically.

The engineer broke into a smile. "You're real railroaders now. There's a trainmen's bunkhouse down by the yard. You can wash up there."

"We'll work hard, sir. You'll see."

They were hired. It was as easy as that. Meg and Jamie retrieved their canvas bags and went out to York Street. As they headed down to the wash house, they happened to see Will Ryan again. He was driving his stage loaded with passengers and luggage. Meg grabbed Jamie's arm, and the two stopped on the boardwalk to watch.

Will was by himself high on the box of the stage. He crouched forward intently, his hands gripping the reins. They could hear him shout, "High up!" to his team. Then the loud, crisp crack of the whip forced the horses into a gallop. The coach skidded around a corner and gathered speed. Again the whip sang, hooves pounded on the hard ground, and a cloud of dust flew up from the big rear

wheels. In a moment the stage had disappeared northward.

"He could get somebody killed, driving like that," said
Meg disapprovingly.

But Jamie's eyes were glowing. "Would I ever like to
drive a stage. It sure would be better than working in a
kitchen."

"What's wrong with kitchen work?"

"It's for girls."

Meg stopped, her hands on her hips. "Is there something the matter with girls?"

"I suppose not, but I want to work on engines or maybe
look after horses — do a man's job."

"You're just afraid of hard work, Jamie Bains."

"I am not! I'm just as ..." But Meg had already turned
away and was heading down the street.

They found the wash house and scrubbed themselves
clean for the first time in a week. Meg changed her clothes
and then combed out her long blonde hair, rewinding it
up into a bun. Jamie put on a fresh shirt, and at his sister's
insistence he slicked down his brown hair with water,
parting it in the middle.

After a meal in a railway cafe on Rectory Street, where
they spent much of the money that Meg had hoarded, they
headed into town. London was a busy, growing city of
25,000 people. Already breweries, tanneries and oil re-
fineries had sprung up, but the place still had a feel of the
frontier. They bought envelopes and writing paper for a
couple of pennies and went off to the Mechanic's Insti-

tute, a type of library and cultural centre for workers, to write home.

"Sure would be nice to see the family again," said Meg as she smoothed the paper out on the desk.

"Maybe they could move to London and we could all get a house?" asked Jamie. "We could manage if we were all together. When Robbie's a bit older I could show him how to sell newspapers and ..."

"It would cost too much money."

"We could use our wages. If we saved ..."

"For heaven's sake, Jamie, be realistic. It would take months for us to save enough for their train trip." Meg shook her head impatiently and turned her attention to the letter. Jamie glared at her but said nothing.

By the time they got back to the railroad yards, Sam Bolt and his crew were making up the train they were to take to the camp. The locomotive was small compared to the ones used for passengers on the main line, but it was a marvel of complicated engineering. The big round boiler had been polished until it was a glossy black, and the thick brass bands that held the seams together gleamed. The cowcatcher in the front was black cast iron. Above it an enormous lamp was attached to the bulbous smokestack. There were four sets of wheels: two small ones in the front, and two gigantic driving wheels located almost under the cab where the pistons were attached. On the side of the tender that carried the cord wood for the hungry fire, the numbers 151 were painted in bright-red letters.

Sam was leaning out of the window watching the hand signals of the switchman. He would back the train up to a boxcar waiting on a siding, slow the engine as he approached, and then, keeping his eyes on the switchman, would bring it almost to a stop. With a gentle nudge the train would make contact with the car, the switchman would hitch it onto the train, and Sam would drive forward again.

Soon the engineer gave a long blast of his steam whistle. "Come on!" he shouted to the crew that had gathered by the side of the tracks. "Climb onto the flatcar back there. We're on our way!"

In moments Jamie and Meg, along with the labourers, swarmed aboard the flatcar. With another long blast the train began to ease forward, switches were thrown, the train went onto the main line, and they were off.

Slowly they gathered speed as they went past the Great Western station. Meg found a spot behind a pile of railroad ties to keep out of the wind, but Jamie sat up on some steel rails to get a better view.

The other workers were a rough crew. Jamie knew that men like this spent most of their time in construction camps or riding the rails in a restless search for work. The pay was never good, the hours were long, and the work brutal.

The men huddled together on the flatcar in groups of twos and threes, talking or dozing off. Once they were in the camp it would be a long time before they would have another soft day like this one.

As they passed the crossings of Richmond, Talbot and Ridout streets, Sam gave blasts of his steam whistle. Then the train was onto the long wooden bridge across the Thames River. Meg and Jamie both peered out over the edge of the flatcar, looking down through the ties, struts and braces to the water a long way below. Once across, they were in the open country gathering speed.

Jamie watched the thick black smoke pouring out of the onion-shaped stack of the engine up ahead. He was not looking forward to the kitchen job. If only he could be an engineer of a locomotive. He imagined himself leaning out the window with the wind in his hair and his hand on the throttle. He wanted to learn about how steam power drove engines, and the inner workings of complicated machinery. Perhaps if he showed Sam Bolt that he was eager to learn, the engineer might agree to explain things.

Up ahead the locomotive whistle gave a long blast as they crossed a road. The train was going twenty miles an hour or more now. They seemed to be rushing through the countryside, past buildings and fields, at breakneck speed. Jamie stood up and began to make his way to the front of the car.

"Where are you going?" Meg called after him.

"Up to the engine."

"You can't do that." She got to her feet and began following him. "It's against the rules." But Jamie ignored her.

At the forward end of the flatcar, the boy paused to look at the ground rushing past. The noise of the steel wheels, squealing and clacking as they hit the rail joints, was deafening. Cautiously he leaned forward, grabbed the ladder of the boxcar that was just ahead and then leapt onto it. In a moment he scrambled up to the top of the car and began making his way forward on the narrow cat-walk.

Meg didn't know what to do. She was sure there had to be rules against going up to the engine, but she couldn't let her brother go alone. She stood at the front of the flatcar and gazed through the gaping space at the ground rushing past. The train rolled and pitched on the uneven track. She hitched up her dress with one hand and leaned forward until she could grab a rung of the ladder on the boxcar. Then with a leap she was onto the ladder and climbing up.

When she peered over the top of the boxcar she could see Jamie a couple of cars ahead. He paused for a moment, then took a quick run and leapt for the next car. Meg's heart almost stopped, but he landed on his feet and kept going.

Meg pulled herself to the roof of the car and stood up. The train rolled like a ship at sea. The wind was rushing at her, tugging at her ankle-length dress as if trying to blow her off the car. Cautiously she made her way forward, keeping to the narrow cat-walk, bending into the wind that howled around her.

When she got to the front of the car she stopped. Ahead of her was a five-foot chasm. The car rocked unsteadily, the wind billowed her dress like a sail, smoke from the engine caught in her throat, and the ground rushed by with dizzying speed. If she jumped and missed, she would fall between the cars and be crushed under the giant steel wheels of the train.

Panic seized her, but she fought against it. Cautiously she backed up, hitched up her long dress with one hand, and concentrated on the open space between the two cars. She sprinted, a cry coming from her throat, then leapt, thinking only about the car ahead. The moment she landed she scrambled to her feet and kept going without looking back.

Four more times she had to jump between the moving boxcars. Each time she knew that if she missed, it would mean certain death. But she pressed on and finally made it to the cab.

"You shouldn't have come forward!" she shouted at Jamie over the noise.

"Sam doesn't mind."

"It is against the rules," the engineer said, looking at them critically.

"You just won't listen, Jamie. Come on, we've got to go back." She turned to the trainman standing at his controls. "I'm sorry, Sam."

"Well, as long as you're here, I guess it's all right."

"See ..." Jamie smiled in triumph.

"But if you're in the cab, you've got to work for your keep. You can help Jay fill the firebox, boy. Hustle to it."

Jamie found it back-breaking work. He had to climb into the tender and wrestle out the four-foot pieces of cord wood which Jay shoved into the ever-hungry fire. They were heavy pieces of maple and birch. It wasn't long before the boy's clothes were filthy, and he was tired.

Sam blew blasts on his whistle. "Hyde Park Junction. This is where we branch off the main line and take the London, Huron and Bruce."

Meg leaned out of the cab window and watched while the switchman wrestled with the big steel arm that changed the track. When it was thrown, a hand signal was given, Sam opened the throttle, and the train switched off the main line and onto the new track heading north.

Now they were passing open fields, concession roads and the occasional farm house. It was rolling country with stands of hardwood, turning a golden yellow and deep red, scattered in among pastures and fields of stubbled grain. Occasionally they went past fields with stacks of hay drying in the late afternoon sun. There was a warmth and prosperity about the land that made it glow.

The train was rolling down the track at little better than a walking pace. "She's not ballasted yet," Sam explained.

"Ballasted?" asked Jamie.

"They've got to pack gravel and cinders and rock all around the ties to hold them down. This track was only laid a few weeks ago. They haven't had time to do it yet."

"If you have to go this slow you'd never beat the stagecoach in a race," said Jamie.

Sam sneered. "Beat him? There's not a team of horses alive that can beat a train over a distance. The railway's bringin' a revolution to this country. It will let farmers market their goods and bring the products of the city out to the countryside. People will be able to read newspapers printed that day. The train is the great civilizer. It's the end of the frontier and the beginning of a new life for these people. The stagecoach is a thing of the past."

Meg was thoughtful. "I guess that's why Will Ryan hates the railroad so much. It would mean the end of his business."

"He's just afraid of the future, that's all."

Once they went through the tiny village of Ilderton, the engineer began opening up the throttle. They were steaming along at a good rate when Sam ordered Jamie to shake loose the smokestack. "Let's see if you've got the makin's of a railroader, boy."

As the wood burned in the firebox, it threw off red-hot cinders. A wire screen was fastened over the top of the smokestack to catch them, but after a while so much accumulated that the smoke could hardly escape.

Sam tied a red scarf around the boy's nose and mouth, making him look like a bandit. Cautiously Jamie went out onto the running board of the engine and crept around the side of the locomotive. The wind was in his face. Trees, fields and farm buildings rushed past, and the train heaved on the uneven track. The boy had never felt such a sensation of speed in all his life.

He bent down and got a long pole that was lashed to the running board. The train rolled and lurched, and he had to be careful not to touch the hot side of the big boiler. The wind surged around him, and the pole was heavy and awkward. It took all his effort, but he managed to manoeuvre it around until he could use it to hit the opening of the stack. With each knock of the pole, more cinders fell back into the firebox. Thick, black smoke came streaming out, catching in his nose and throat despite his mask. Cautiously Jamie put the pole back in place and made his way back to the cab.

Sam was laughing. "Shakin' down the cinders is the true test, boy." Jamie beamed.

The town of Brecon was down in a bit of a hollow. As they approached, Sam opened the throttle and blew a long warning blast. By the time they got to the bottom of the dip, it seemed as if they were flying. Sam hollered for more steam. Jay threw cord wood into the flaming inferno, slamming the door shut as quickly as possible. The engine roared and chugged its way up the grade until, with what seemed like a supreme effort, the train crested the hill.

They were doing twenty-five, maybe thirty miles an hour. The big wheels hammered on the rail joints, the hitches rattled and the boiling water in the engines seethed violently. When Jay opened the fire door to feed the flames, a blast of red heat leapt out at them.

As they went through the village of Clandeboye, Sam barely slackened his speed. At the crossing of the main street of town he blew a long, shrieking blast on his whistle. Meg saw a horse hitched to a carriage suddenly rear up in fright and paw the air with its front hooves. People on the street stopped to watch the speeding freight train. Children ran after them. Dogs barked wildly. Sam just laughed and opened his throttle further.

"We're gonna get there in record time," he shouted happily.

It was already beginning to get dark, but still Sam coaxed his locomotive faster and faster. The line ran a hundred yards or more to the west of the London-Goderich highway. From his position in the tender, handing cord wood to the fireman, Jamie could see wagons and carriages out on the road. The train steamed by them like they were standing still. The farms and trees hurtled past.

Suddenly Sam was leaning out of his window. "There's somethin' on the line!!"

Meg looked out the left side of the cab. A dark, massive object lay across the track a hundred yards ahead.

In an instant Sam cut his throttle and frantically blew the down-brake signal on the whistle. "It's a tree!" Again he blew the desperate signal to the brakeman.

Already the big driving wheels were screaming on the tracks as Sam cut the power. But the tree still hurtled towards them at a terrible speed.

"More brakes!" Sam screamed, and he gave a desperate blast on the whistle again. "We need all the brakes we've got, or we'll never stop in time!"

Each of the freight cars had its own brakes, and the brakeman, stationed in the caboose, would be up on top of the train turning them down.

Jay, the fireman, leapt for the back of the tender and turned down its brake wheel. The armstrongs, as they called the brakes on the freight cars, were iron wheel-like affairs that stood a couple of feet over the top of the car.

"Stop! Damn you, stop!!" The engineer screamed at his train. Again he frantically blew his brake signal.

But they were coming too fast. The train rushed on. Meg watched the enormous object on the track grow larger and larger.

"Hold on!!!"

The locomotive hit the tree with a bone-wrenching jar. Iron and steel crushed and crumpled. Glass shattered. Steam hissed. Wood, thrown about in the tender, sounded like an avalanche. Somewhere a bell was clanging incessantly.

The engine mounted up onto the tree, tipped slowly, teetered for a moment, and then fell onto its side. The two boxcars immediately behind twisted with the engine and fell with a shattering sound of splintering wood and metal.

CHAPTER 3

"JAMIE, where are you!?" Meg's voice mounted into a shriek.

Steam was escaping from the big boiler with a whistling sound. The door to the firebox had flown open and the flames made a red glow in the darkened cab.

"Jamie!! Jamie!! ... Are you all right?"

The engine lay on its side like a big, beached whale. The boiling water in her tank steamed and gurgled as if she still had some life in her, but the beast was wounded and close to death.

Everything in the cab was turned over and spewed about in complete disorder. The growing darkness made it hard to see, and now Meg found herself groping through the wreckage. "Jamie! ... Jamie!!"

Something stirred in the cab. Rubble was cast aside and a big form rose up. "Damn ... !!" Sam Bolt cursed. "Damn stinkin' tree!" He pulled himself up to his full height.

"Sam, have you seen Jamie?"

The engineer rubbed the side of his head. "Watch you don't get burned on the steam there, girl. Careful of the fire!" He eased Meg aside with an arm and swung the firedoor shut. Then he closed all the dampers to smother the flames.

"Jamie! Where is he?" Tears were flowing down the girl's face now. She had to find her brother.

"He was in the tender with the wood!"

Awkwardly Meg pulled herself through the door of the cab and looked inside the tender. Long pieces of firewood were strewn about in a great tangled pile. Some were still in the tender while others had spilled out onto the ground.

"Jamie!" the girl called, but in the dim light she couldn't see a sign of him. "He must be under the wood! Sam, help me, please!"

Meg scrambled onto the ground and began tearing at the jumble of logs with her hands. Sam leapt down beside her and pulled at the timbers, throwing them aside in a desperate attempt to find the boy.

"Jamie!!" Meg screamed in despair. "Jamie!!!"

"Over here, Meg! I'm over here!" The voice came from the ditch beside an overturned boxcar several yards away.

Meg ran to her brother. "Jamie ... Jamie ... I thought ... !" She felt such incredible relief that she couldn't control her tears.

"It's Jay, the fireman. He's hurt." The boy was crouched over the moaning shape of a man.

The fireman's face was an ashen grey. Beneath him his legs were twisted.

"What happened?"

"When we crashed, I was thrown clear, but ... "

Sam rushed over and other men from the flatcar at the end of the train came running up.

"Jay was on top of the boxcar turning down the brakes," Jamie said. "He must have been thrown off when it went over. I think he's broken both his legs."

The engineer bent down over the crumpled form of his fireman. "My God ... Jay. What have I done to you!" Sam looked up at the anxious crowd around him. "He's hurt! Hurt bad. We've got to get help!"

"Blankets," someone shouted. "There must be some in the caboose." Two of the men sprinted for the end of the train. "Look for a stretcher!" another called after them.

Tears were gathering in Sam's eyes. Meg put her arm on the engineer's arm. "It wasn't your fault."

He looked up at the girl. "I was going too fast."

"The tree fell across the track. It was an accident."

"If Jay dies, I ... " The big engineer gently stroked Jay's face. "We worked together ... drank together. We were like brothers."

The men were back with a stack of blankets. "He's in shock," someone said. "We've got to get him to a doctor."

Con Lucas, the conductor, rushed up. Sam got to his feet to explain what happened. By the time he had finished, he appeared more collected.

Two men were dispatched to a farm house they could see a hundred yards or more over on the highway. Sam gave specific instructions. "We need the farmer's best horse and wagon to take Jay to the doctor in Exeter. The town can't be more than a mile away. Tell him the railway will pay good money, but he's got to hurry."

Sam looked around at the men assembled and pointed at the youngest. "The camp ... the construction camp ...

it's about three miles north of here. You can't miss it. Tell them to bring the other train and to hurry."

"I'm goin'!" The man took off at a sprint.

There was no stretcher on the train, so two of the men made one out of a blanket and two poles they cut out of the bush. When they finished, they set the stretcher alongside the injured fireman.

The shadows had lengthened, and the darkness was gathering. The faces of those around the injured man were pale and strained.

Gently one of the men tried to straighten the twisted legs. A painful shriek shattered the air.

"Stop! Stop!!" shouted Meg.

Jay's eyes opened and shut without focusing. "Sam...!" cracked his voice. "Sam ... !!"

"Don't touch his legs!!" The girl was emphatic. Everyone was looking at her. "It could injure him even more badly."

Jay moaned and drifted into unconsciousness.

Meg crouched down beside him and tried to speak calmly. "Jamie, get me that stick. That's it." Gently she pried open his mouth and put the inch-thick stick between his teeth. "Sam, hold this so he doesn't bite his tongue."

The engineer watched her anxiously.

"Put the stretcher there beside him." The men laid their improvised blanket and poles beside Jay and waited for more instructions from the girl.

"We have to roll him onto his side to get the stretcher under him." Meg and others began to ease him over. "That's it. Careful of his legs!"

Cries of pain were muffled. Jay's body trembled and shook uncontrollably. Then he slipped into unconsciousness. Gently they eased him onto his back with the stretcher under him. Meg took two blankets and spread them over him to keep him warm. When she was finished, the men lifted the stretcher up onto level ground.

"That's all we can do until he sees the doctor," Meg said.

The twilight had deepened into complete darkness. A half moon had risen over the horizon, casting an eerie glow over the scene, but the shadows were so deep that they were impenetrable. In a couple of minutes they heard the heavy stomp of hooves, and the wagon arrived.

The farmer shook his head when he saw the train wreck. "Always knew that iron horse would be trouble," he drawled, tugging on his straw hat.

Carefully the men loaded Jay into the flat bed of the hay rack. Con Lucas and one of the labourers were sent along to ride with him to the doctor.

After they had left, Sam turned back to his train and began a thorough inspection of the damage. Someone found a couple of lanterns and a torch in the caboose.

The engine had ridden up onto the tree and then tipped over on its side, pulling the two boxcars with it. The other cars and the caboose still stood upright on the track.

It was the engine that Sam was most concerned about. The train had not been going very fast when it hit, and the tree had eased its fall so the boiler had not erupted, but the front part of the locomotive was smashed. The cowcatcher was a twisted wreck, the lantern was junk and various attachments were bent out of shape.

The water in the boiler had cooled somewhat. Sam took one of the lanterns and rummaged around in the wreck of the cab until he found a big wrench. Carefully he opened two valves on the boiler, and the water slowly began draining.

The two boxcars were a mess. The cars were made out of wood, and they had been shattered into splinters. One of the cars had carried railroad ties that were spewed in a tangled mass by the side of the track. The other car had carried provisions for the camp. In among its rubble were sacks of beans, oatmeal and flour. A side of beef and dozens of chickens lay in the dirt along with smashed eggs, butter and half a dozen large barrels.

"Looks like a total loss," commented Jamie, nimbly climbing over the rubble.

"Could be a lot worse," Sam replied. "The wheels on the boxcars and the undercarriage are all right. They can rebuild the rest, and the engine can be repaired."

By the time they had finished their inspection, they heard the train from the construction camp coming towards them. The huge lantern of a locomotive coming from the north penetrated the night. On the running board of the engine and the flatcar pulled behind were thirty or more men carrying lanterns and torches that sent huge yellow flames into the air. When the train stopped on the other side of the fallen tree, men swarmed towards them.

"What happened, Sam?" The men milled around the wrecked locomotive, their torches and lanterns giving a ghostly illumination to the scene.

"The tree was across the track. I couldn't stop in time. Jay Brown is badly injured. They've taken him into Exeter."

"Sam," someone was calling. "Sam, did you see this?"

"What?"

"The tree. Didn't you look at it?"

The men circled the base of the tree, the flames dancing in their hands.

"I think it might have been cut," the man said. "Aren't those axe marks at the roots there?"

"Could be," said another.

Sam grabbed a torch out of someone's hand and bent down to inspect the tree trunk. When he straightened up, his face was grim. "The Ryans dropped the tree across the track."

"The Ryans?"

"The stagecoach men who run the line between London and Exeter. They're lookin' for ways to stop the railroad 'cause we're gonna ruin their business."

"You mean they chopped the tree down on purpose?"

The flames gave a gleam to Sam's face. "They're killers!"

"Look. Fresh tracks." Torches were held high so they could see. "There was a horse all over here."

"Maybe they cut the roots and then pulled the tree over with their horses to make it look like it had just fallen down."

"The Ryans did it!" Sam was in a fury. "When I turned down their foolish race they vowed they were going to get us. Murderers, that's what they are!!"

"But we don't know it's them," Jamie said weakly. "Those are just some marks around the roots. The tree wasn't cut right through and ... and maybe it fell over by itself. I don't know ... "

"Look what happened to Jay Brown. A braver railroad man you'll never find. Up on top of the car ... tryin' to turn down the brakes ... thrown off and his body smashed. You saw his twisted legs. Broken! Maybe crippled for life! And who did it? The Ryans! I know that in my bones!"

"We can't let them get away with it!" someone shouted.

The circle of flaming torches danced brilliantly. In the centre, Sam Bolt was shaking. "Jay Brown was my friend. I'm not going to sit by and let the Ryans get away with this."

There was silence as Sam looked around at the men. When he spoke again, his voice was low. "I know this. Every day the Ryans drive their stage down the Proof Line Road on the London-Exeter run and every night the brothers gather in a saloon in Exeter. They'll be there now ... drinkin' back the whisky ... bragging to everyone how they stopped the railway."

Sam's face gleamed with sweat. He turned slowly and looked at the forty men or more who stood around him in the circle of flickering torch light. "Well, I aim to put a stop to it. I intend to get them Ryans for what they did to

Jay so that they won't ever think to do something like this to railroad men again."

"Yeah, Sam," came the voices out of the dark.

"Let's do it."

"Get them Ryans once and for all."

"But you don't know it's them for sure, Sam," Jamie repeated meekly. "You can't go accusing them without … "

"You saw what they did to Jay! You were there!!" the engineer was shouting.

"But … "

"We're doin' this for Jay Brown and the railroad. This'll be the last wreck the Ryans ever make. Come on! We're goin' into Exeter!"

With Sam in the lead, the mob of men headed towards town. Meg looked at her brother, uncertain what to do. Then the two of them ran to catch up.

CHAPTER 4

THE crowd of men surged along a small wagon track to the main road and then turned towards the town of Exeter. They were a mass of darkened forms, carrying torches and lanterns that flickered in the night.

Engineer Sam Bolt was at the front of the mob, holding a blazing flame high above his head. He walked quickly, his fury forcing his legs into long strides. Behind him came the railroaders.

The autumn half moon had risen into a cloudless sky, casting a pale light on the fields and forests. Stars in their thousands had come out. In the distance they could see the lights of the town. Hurry as they might, Jamie and Meg could do no more than keep up with the back of the procession.

The mob entered the town along Main Street from the south. In the outskirts, scattered buildings were on both sides of the road. Then the houses were closer together and finally, in the business section of the town, the shops were built in long attached rows. Almost every one of the buildings showed candle and lantern lights weakly shining through the windows. In some places people came to watch the crowd of men passing in the night.

Exeter was a market town serving the surrounding farming district. The country had been settled less than fifty years earlier, but already it had gained some prosperity and was leaving its frontier past behind. Some of the houses were white-brick, two-storey buildings, but others were built of squared log. In the centre of town, shops had large display windows trimmed with fancy woodwork. A boardwalk a few feet wide extended out from buildings, and most places had a hitching post for horses. At the main intersection two gas streetlamps gave a pale illumination.

The railroad men filled the gravel road from side to side, their boots stirring up a cloud of dust. The lights of their torches and lanterns gleamed in the reflection of the shop windows.

"There it is," Sam called. "The Exeter Hotel. That's where the Ryans hang out."

The hotel was a substantial establishment for a small town. It was built on a street corner and had a broad porch along the two outer walls. The posts and railings were painted white, and the double doors that led into the saloon bar were stained a dark colour. Most of the windows on the ground floor of the hotel were open, and inside they could hear the sound of talking and laughter.

The crowd of men surged forward, but at a signal from Sam they stopped and stood in the street facing the hotel. Slowly they became silent.

Sam was in the centre of the men, two steps in front of the others. Meg and Jamie stood nervously on the fringes.

"Will Ryan!" Sam shouted. "Will Ryan! Are you in there?"

The saloon grew quiet. Men came to peer out the windows and then disappeared again.

"Ryan! We want to talk to you!" The engineer's voice seemed to fill the streets.

"What do you want?" came a voice from one of the windows.

"We want the Ryan boys."

"Who are you?"

"We're the railroaders. There's been trouble on the line, and the Ryans caused it."

It was quiet inside the saloon and on the street. The railroaders were big, determined men. For the first time Jamie noticed that some of them carried shovels. Others had long-handled hammers used to drive in spikes; one carried a pickaxe. They waited, restlessly shifting from foot to foot.

A minute passed, and then another. Sam was impatient. "Come out here, Ryan, or we're gonna come in after you."

The lanterns inside the saloon went out, and windows slammed shut.

"Let's go in and get 'em," one of the railroaders said.

"Bet they've escaped through the back door."

"Chicken-livered cowards."

"Ryan," Sam shouted again. "If we gotta come in after you that hotel will be some sorry sight afterwards."

There was the sound of movement inside. Slowly the double doors of the hotel opened, and four men stepped out onto the porch. They came to the top step and glared down at the railroaders on the street below.

Will Ryan wore his heavy brown suit and big coachman's boots. His black curly hair shone in the light. Bobby stood beside him with a smile on his face. The two men with them were as big and square as the others. One had a neatly trimmed moustache; another, long sideburns.

Will leaned casually against a porch post. "Whatcha want, railroad man?"

The light from a flaming torch danced in Sam's hand. "I want your hide." His voice growled.

"You ain't man enough to get it."

"These your brothers?"

"Yeah, the Ryan clan: Frank, Tom and you know Bobby. He's the youngest and wildest of the family. You want to tangle with us?"

"No one's stupid enough to mess with the Ryan boys," said Bobby with a laugh.

Will was smiling. "This here's Sam Bolt, boys. He's the engineer on that rail line who blows his steam whistle at horses every chance he gets."

"And you're the Ryan boys who drop trees across the railway track," Sam snapped angrily.

"What are you sayin'?"

"You know what I'm talkin' about."

"I know nothin' 'bout railways."

Sam took a step towards the porch. The flame in his hand made his face gleam. "This afternoon you sent your brothers out to the rail line, and they pulled a big maple tree across the track."

"You accusin' us of some crime, mister?" asked Bobby belligerently.

"That's right. I'm accusin'."

"And what proof you got?"

Sam turned and handed his torch to one of the men behind him. When he faced the Ryan boys again his hands were closed into fists.

"We hit that tree and one of my men broke both his legs, maybe worse."

Will showed no expression. "Should drive more careful, like."

"You caused that accident!"

"You got nothin' on us."

"Just watchin' the way you act gives me all the proof I need." Sam's finger was pointing. "You wanted to get back at me 'cause I wouldn't race your stagecoach. Maybe you were still mad over the time I scared your horses. I don't know. But just as sure as I'm standin' here you and your brothers were the ones who dropped the tree, and I'm gonna make you pay for what you did to my fireman."

"Then come ahead."

Meg grasped her brother's hand. Something terrible was about to happen, and she didn't know how to stop it.

Sam turned to his men. "All right! We've had enough of this chatter. Let's get 'em!!" A throaty roar came from the railway men.

Suddenly a revolver exploded. Dust spurted up at Sam's feet. A smoking gun was in Will Ryan's hand.

"Another step, and you're a dead man, Bolt," the stage driver said calmly.

All of the Ryan boys had guns in their hands now. Steadily, almost lazily, they swept their weapons across the crowd.

The railroaders stood rooted to the spot.

"Come on, mister engineer." Will Ryan beckoned him with his free hand. "Come ahead, but this gun will go off, and I'll have to call it self-defense."

Sam and the others were paralyzed.

"You come into town here, with a mob behind you, accusin' me and my brothers of all manner of lies. You say you're gonna spread us all over the street." He laughed. "Only time you're brave is when you've got a crowd behind you."

Will stuck his revolver into his belt. He slouched up against a pillar, folded his arms and leered down at the men in the street. The railroaders waited, unable to tear themselves away.

"Now let me give you a little bit of advice, Sam Bolt. And the rest of you railroaders had better listen good, 'cause it might save you a pile of trouble." Will paused for a moment. "From Exeter down through Lucan to London belongs to the Ryan boys. You remember that. We're good folk. A little wild, maybe ... out for a good time on a Saturday night, but otherwise we're upstanding citizens. Isn't that right, boys?" The brothers smiled.

"But there's a couple of things us Ryans won't put up with. One is we won't have a mob musclin' their way into our town, accusin' us of something we have nothin' to do

with. The other is we won't have nobody or nothin'
interferin' with our stage line. That's our livelihood, and
we're gonna keep it. You understand?"

Will Ryan paused and looked around. It was quiet on
the street. The flames of the torches had burned down.
Some had even gone out, and the spent sticks had been
thrown on the ground.

"Now you'd better clear out, but remember. We're not
gonna stand by and be buried under that iron horse."

Will and his brothers gave one more contemptuous
look at the defeated men on the street, opened the big
doors to the hotel, and disappeared inside.

The railroaders stirred restlessly. Men whispered
together and then slowly groups of two and three began
to head back down the dusty road. Soon all the men were
walking together back to the train, leaving Sam standing
on the street. A few paces away lingered Meg and Jamie.

The engineer stared at the ground without moving.

"Sam," Meg called softly. "Sam … "

He looked up. His round face seemed pale and drained.
"Yeah."

"We have to get back to the train before they leave
without us."

They started following the others. Soon the darkness
enveloped them. Overhead the moon had become a pale
half-disc surrounded by millions of stars.

"It's a disaster," muttered the engineer, more to himself than anyone else. "The engine's damaged, two boxcars have been smashed, Jay's been injured, perhaps

permanently, and I back down before thòse Ryan thugs in front of all the men."

Meg put her hand on his arm. "It's not so bad."

Sam looked at her curiously, and she smiled at him. "We've learned a lot about the Ryan boys," she said. "Maybe next time we'll be better prepared for them."

CHAPTER 5

BY the time they got back to the site of the train wreck, the locomotive from the construction camp was being fired up. Jamie, Meg and the others barely had time to get their gear and climb aboard a flatcar before they set off for the camp. The train travelled cautiously through the night, until finally a huge white tent, glowing from lanterns burning inside, loomed out of the dark. They slowed and came to a stop.

"Come on," said Sam to Meg and Jamie. "I'll introduce you to your new boss."

The railroaders piled off the train and headed into the big cook tent. Inside, it was dimly lit with coal-oil lanterns and filled with long tables and benches where the men ate. Along one side were stoves and huge washtubs.

Jamie and Meg hadn't eaten since noon. A delicious smell of baked beans and bread hung about the place, making them all the more famished.

A tall man wearing a big white apron and carrying a ladle was shouting in a loud voice over the noise. "All you men who ate your dinner high-tail it outta here. You new men get yourself a plate, and serve up what slim pickin's is left."

The men milled about the tent, keeping a respectable distance from the cook as if afraid they might get a whack from his wooden ladle. He was an intimidating man: gaunt, slim and cavernous with piercing blue eyes and an irritable look on his face.

"Mr. Henry," Sam called as he walked towards the cook. "I've got you a couple of new recruits for your kitchen."

The tall man looked at Meg and Jamie critically. "Children to work for me?"

"Hired 'em this mornin'. It'll free up a couple more men to lay track."

"Is the railway hirin' children to do a man's work? Girls in long dresses, and a boy so small he don't look like he could lift a pail of water." As he spoke, Mr. Henry felt Jamie's arm and shoulder as if evaluating a side of beef. "Here I got to feed two hundred hungry gandy dancers, and they send me this ... "

"You saying we can't work?" Meg was bristling.

"If you work for Mr. Henry, you'll put sweat on your brow. I'll tell you that. I won't have girls who spend their days tryin' to look pretty, and young boys who head out fishin'."

"We can work with the best of them."

"We'll see. The two of you had better get tucked into some grub there, and then get some shut eye. Wake-up time's five o'clock in the mornin' for kitchen help, and you'd best be ready."

"We'll be there," promised Meg.

The two of them got tin bowls and filled them out of a big pot that simmered on the stove. They sat by themselves at one of the long tables and spooned up the beans and thick chunks of salt pork swimming in a sweet brown sauce. Big loaves of freshly baked bread were on the table. They tore off chunks and smeared it with soft yellow butter.

After they had eaten, they cleared away their dishes and cutlery, put them in a big wash bucket and followed the bull cook that Mr. Henry had sent to find them a place to sleep.

Meg presented a problem. The labourers slept in boxcars converted into bunkhouses that were parked on a siding, but a young girl couldn't sleep in the same room as a group of men. She also wasn't a foreman, eligible for a private room. Finally, after some shifting around, the bull cook found them a small cubicle in the trainman's car.

Their sleeping quarters were no more than a cubbyhole with a set of bunks in it, but they didn't care. They were so exhausted that they would have slept in a ditch. Jamie lit a candle and set it in a small holder while Meg spread blankets over the bare mattresses.

"I don't like the look of that Mr. Henry," Jamie muttered. "He seems like a hard man to me."

"He'll be all right. You'll see. Let's get to bed. Tomorrow's going to come pretty early."

"But the kitchen ... " The boy gave a big sigh. "If only I could get on the construction gang, or do some sort of man's work."

When he had climbed into the top bunk, his sister blew out the candle and crept under the rough blanket in the bottom. They were quiet for a few moments before Meg said, "I wonder how Mother and the kids are doing?"

"I hope they're not going hungry," Jamie spoke into the darkness. "We should be there to help them. Kate and Rob aren't big enough to look after themselves."

"We're doing all we can."

"I just wish … "

"What?"

"Oh, never mind. You wouldn't understand."

"What do you mean, I wouldn't understand?" Meg said sharply. "I miss them, too." They were silent for a few moments before she added. "I think they'll be all right. Jamie … ? Jamie … ?" But he was asleep.

The wake-up call seemed to come before they had time to roll over. "Come on, you two. Feet on the floor. We've got a whole herd of hungry men to feed." It was Mr. Henry himself.

They were out of bed, dressed, washed and at work in ten minutes. The cook rode them with a constant nattering. "Build up the fire there, girl. Be quick about it. Boy, there's a couple of pails out behind the tent. Go across to the pump at the farmer's building over there. We need at least four full pails of water. Jump to 'er now."

And work they did. For the next hour they were hauling water, pouring it into big vats on the cook stove, and when it was boiling, dumping in bags of oatmeal. Then they had to stir the stuff with ladles as large as paddles and watch to see it didn't burn on the bottom. Mr. Henry was busy baking dozens of loaves of bread.

The first wake-up call for the workers was at six, and in moments men began to come out of the boxcars to get washed. Soon dozens of hungry men were in the cook tent waiting to be fed.

The railroad provided food for their construction workers for a fee deducted from their wages. It was plain cooking, but the men expected to be given as much as they wanted. That morning big bowls of porridge were put out on the tables, along with huge jugs of milk and blackstrap molasses. Loaves of bread, still hot from the oven, were smeared with thick yellow butter and sweet jam. Everything was washed down with cups of strong tea.

Mr. Henry ruled his cook tent with an iron fist. He prowled the alleyways between the tables watching the manners of the men. When food was running low at one of the tables, he would give a shout, and Meg or Jamie would hurry to bring another loaf of bread or steaming bowl of porridge. Any of the men who made a mess or a commotion could expect a stiff lecture, and anyone who dared complain was taking his life into his hands. The cook would bellow a curse and then come out with a stream of abuse that could curl the hair on a hound dog.

Jamie was on edge from the beginning. The cook shouted at him constantly, and when he couldn't deliver the order immediately, lectures came hot and fast. "Jump to it now, boy, or you'll be takin' the next train back south." The cook glared at him with piercing blue eyes.

"I can't do everything at once," the boy tried to explain nervously.

"No excuses for a laggard. Now work!"

Sam Bolt sat at a table with the foremen. As it got close to the seven o'clock starting time, the men cleared away their dirty dishes and went outside to wait for instructions.

Meg and Jamie could hear the camp boss giving out his orders in a loud voice. "I'm sending thirty men with Sam Bolt to clean up that wreck. The rest of you get out to work. We've got a railway to build and lost time to make up."

There was a confusion of noise and equipment as the work was organized. A telegram was sent to headquarters in London to tell Mr. Mason, the superintendent, about the accident. Men were dispatched to get tools, horses were hitched up to wagons and made off for either the wreck or the end of the steel, and the construction locomotive got up a head of steam. When everything was ready, the engine gave a blast of its whistle, the workers swarmed aboard the flatcars, and the train left to travel the couple of miles back to the accident site.

Jamie stood at the front of the cook tent, wishing that he was going with the men.

"All right there, lad, get away from that doorway," came a sharp voice from behind him. "There won't be no lazin' about when you're workin' for Mr. Henry." Jamie rushed back to his chores as if he had been stung.

Jamie and Meg had to clear the tables and then wash them down with soap and water. The dishes had to be scraped and stacked and, when the water was steaming on the stove, the two of them had to pour it into big corrugated-iron tubs. Meg volunteered to do the washing. Soon her hands were hot and sore from being in the water for so long.

Jamie was sent again and again to the water pump. When he struggled back with the heavy pails, he had to climb onto a chair and pour the water into the vats on the stove. There was firewood to haul, food to bring out of the larder, and bread dough to knead. The work never seemed to end.

After the washing, Meg and Jamie prepared vegetables for the stew that Mr. Henry was making. It was a long, boring job that Jamie hated. One potato after another — there seemed to be no end to them. Then there were onions, carrots, leeks, parsnips and turnips to peel and cut up. After the vegetables were finished, Mr. Henry gave them big slabs of meat to cut into cubes.

Jamie wasn't very good at the work. He was slow and often wasted too much for the cook's liking. Mr. Henry watched him closely and kept up his constant nagging.

When they had finally finished, the cook called the two of them over. "She's gettin' close to noon, and we're gonna have to take some lunch up to the men at the wreck. Collect some grub together, and I'll get a teamster to haul it up to them."

"I can drive a horse and wagon," said Meg casually.

"You can?"

"She knows everything there is about horses," bragged Jamie. "And I do, too."

"You do not," said his sister.

"I do so!"

"Go and hitch up a horse and wagon, girl. You can haul the lunch up to the men."

"Can I go, too?" asked Jamie hopefully.

"No, I need you here."

"But ... "

"You just want to get out of work, boy. I know your type."

"It's not that. It's just that I ... "

"You're not goin' nowhere, and that's final!"

"Meg ... ?" Jamie turned to his sister.

"You stay here. I won't be gone for long," Meg said abruptly.

The boy turned away as quickly as he could so she would not see the tears gathering in his eyes. Why couldn't she stick up for him?

"I'm warnin' you, boy. You'd best bend your back into this here work, or you'll see trouble from Mr. Henry."

Meg went off to hitch up a horse and rig while Jamie helped get the food together. When the girl returned a few minutes later, they carried the big packages out, placed them carefully in the back of the wagon and covered the food with a large sheet of oilcloth. All the time they worked, Jamie refused to say a word to his sister. It wasn't fair that he was trapped in the camp.

"All right, girl. Get a move on and get your hide back here as soon as lunch is over," Mr. Henry ordered. "We've got lots to do to get that there stew ready for supper."

She bounded up onto the seat of the wagon, slapped the reins across the horse's back, and was off.

There was a wagon track following the railway line, and Meg drove the horse along it at an easy gait. It was a beautiful, warm fall day. The sun was high in a pale-blue sky filled with puffy clouds. Crickets and grasshoppers sang, making the air hum like it was alive. Groundhogs sunned themselves by their burrows, and overhead a hawk circled slowly.

The country was very flat, and on both sides rich farmland stretched as far as she could see. The grain fields had been harvested, and hay was gathered into stooks for drying. Cattle huddled in the shade of the trees or lay on the ground chewing their cuds, trying to stay cool.

In fifteen minutes Meg spotted the train wreck up ahead. She saw that the men had already accomplished a lot. The tree had been cut and hauled away and much of the rubble had been cleared up. The food that had been in one of the cars was stacked in piles waiting to be taken to camp. As she got close she could see that Sam was rigging up a complicated block and tackle system to lift the engine back onto the track.

"Grub's up!" men shouted as they spotted the wagon.

Meg wheeled the wagon around the fallen tree and reined to a stop. She tied off the horse so it could graze on grass, and then climbed into the back of the wagon to help hand out the food.

Everyone was hungry. The men had worked five solid hours at heavy labour in the outdoors, and it had given them huge appetites. Mr. Henry had packed bread, chunks of cooked beef, big jugs of milk, and plenty of apples, peaches and pears. The men dug in.

Sam smiled at Meg when he came up to the wagon. His face was red, and his blue cotton shirt was stained dark with perspiration.

"How's Jay Brown? Do you know?" Meg asked.

"Doctor says he's gonna be all right. Two broken legs. Broke bad, they are, but his innards is all right. It'll be awhile before he's up and around."

"I'm glad he'll be all right."

Sam had sliced off some bread and a chunk of meat. He helped himself to a cup of milk and then settled down on the ground beside the tree. After Meg had covered the food with the oilcloth to keep the flies away, she got something to eat and joined him.

"Are you still sure that it was the Ryans who dropped the tree across the track?" she asked.

"Who else could it be? Those Ryans are tryin' to drive the railway out of the country. You saw Will in London, and then the way they acted last night. They're as guilty as a fox in a hen house."

Meg ate thoughtfully. "But you can't just accuse people without proof."

"This is the frontier out here, girl. We do things our way."

They had just finished lunch when the quiet of the warm afternoon was broken by the sharp blast of a locomotive steam whistle. A train had arrived from the south bringing the superintendent, George Mason.

Sam and Con Lucas, the conductor, hurried over to see him. Then the three men toured the wreck, inspecting the damage. Meg began loading the wagon with the plates and dishes while the workers waited for fresh instructions.

"The tree was right across the track," Sam was explaining. "If we'd hit her any harder, it would have made a terrible wreck."

"And you're sure it was no accident."

"Positive, Mr. Mason. Those Ryan boys must have cut the roots, got a rope around the tree and pulled her over with their horses. We saw the hoof prints."

"Well, I'm going to inform the authorities," announced the superintendent.

"The police won't do nothin'. You know that."

"You shouldn't have gone into town, Sam. I won't have my men making up a vigilante committee." Mr. Mason was very stern.

"Jay was hurt. We had to do something."

The three men were wandering back to the wagon. The labourers got to their feet and gathered around. Mason paused for a moment and looked at the assembled crowd. Then he addressed them with a voice of authority.

"It was a terrible thing that happened here last night. One of our men was seriously injured, and railway property was damaged."

He paused to look around at the wreck behind him. Flies buzzed overhead.

"Someone caused the wreck," he continued. "We don't know for sure who, but we aim to find out. The railway is offering a reward of two hundred dollars to anyone who can find who did it and put a stop to it. Two hundred dollars. That's a lot of money. We hope someone claims it."

CHAPTER 6

BACK at the camp, Jamie worked under the lash of Mr. Henry's sharp tongue. Just before the crew came in for lunch, he was assigned to fill huge soup serving bowls. Then he carried them, one at a time, to the tables. They were heavy, and it was all he could do to hold them steady. More than once soup slopped over the side and splattered onto the ground.

"Can't you even do a simple job?" Mr. Henry shouted.

But it was while he was carrying the bread to the tables that real trouble struck. Jamie had five loaves stacked up in his arms when he tripped. The three on the top went flying onto the ground.

Mr. Henry slammed down the big wooden ladle he was holding. "That does it. I've never seen the likes of someone as clumsy as you."

"It was an accident, sir."

"There are too many accidents with you, boy. I've half a mind to turf you out now."

"Please, just give me a chance."

"I've given you lots of chances." The fury in the tall man frightened Jamie. "I'm not gonna put up with this much longer. Now you go out and ring the bell to call the men for lunch, and you get to thinkin' what a poor job you're doin' here. Understand?"

Jamie rang the big triangle bell so loudly that the ringing hurt his ears. He was furious at Mr. Henry, but he knew he had to watch what he said. They desperately needed this job with the railway.

The men had eaten their lunch and cleared out of the cook tent when Meg bustled in full of excitement. Jamie was washing the dishes.

"You know what?" she said to her brother. "Mr. Mason has promised a two hundred dollar reward to anyone who can find who was responsible for the train wreck."

"Two hundred dollars?"

"If we could get that reward, it would solve all our problems. Mother could move to London. We could be together again. All we need is proof."

"But how are we going to do that?"

"If we can find out about the Ryans, maybe ... "

"I don't see why everyone's so sure the Ryans dropped the tree across the track."

"They're the ones who want to stop the railroad."

"But it could have been anyone, and maybe the tree just fell over by itself. Sam was going too fast to stop. It was partly his fault." Jamie glanced towards the cook. "I've got to get back to work. Mr. Henry is watching me like a hawk." He dipped his hands into the hot water, pulled out one of the plates and angrily began washing it.

Meg seemed lost in thought. "It's got to be the Ryans. We've just got to prove it. That's the hard part."

Mr. Henry was striding towards them. "All right, you've had enough of a holiday," the cook barked. "Jamie hasn't done enough work today to fill two hours. Now get moving!"

The boy busied himself washing the dishes. Meg dried and stacked them. When the cook stepped out of the tent for a moment, she whispered. "Are you causing trouble, Jamie?"

"No!" The boy was annoyed. "Mr. Henry just doesn't like me."

"But if he's complaining about your work ... "

"Listen, I've been working hard since we got up this morning. I didn't get a chance to go out for a ride like you."

"But, Jamie, if we lose these jobs ... "

"I am working hard, Meg. I always work hard. You take his side. You're just not fair!" He threw the wash cloth into the soapy water, making a big splash that wet the table and a bench. Guiltily he hurried to mop it up before the cook returned.

The work seemed unending. They washed the stacks of dirty dishes and then helped mix more bread dough and bake pies for the evening meal. Meg got along reasonably well with Mr. Henry despite his gruff ways, but the best Jamie could do was try to stay out of his way. Finally, in mid-afternoon, they were given a couple of hours off.

"Be back here by four-thirty at the latest," Mr. Henry warned. "There's still lots to do before supper is ready."

"I'm done in. Let's go and have a nap," said Meg to her brother as they were going out of the cook tent.

The boy didn't even look at her. "I'm going to go down and watch them laying track," he muttered.

"Do you want me to come with you?"

"I don't care."

Meg stopped with her hands on her hips. "Are you still mad at me, Jamie?"

"You go off and leave me with that slave driver and don't even stick up for me."

"But you've got to work."

"I do work," he shouted. The boy turned and walked quickly away towards the end of the steel.

"Jamie . . . . " Meg followed her brother for a moment. "Jamie ... come on." But he kept on going without looking back.

It was a good half-mile walk to the head of the steel, and there was lots to see on the way. Men were unloading ties from boxcars onto wagons. It required brute strength, but the labourers heaved the heavy wooden logs easily. Down the track, about fifteen men were unloading steel rails from a flatcar, sliding the rails down wooden skids onto a wagon. Then he came across a crew of men filling the spaces between the ties with a ballast of gravel.

When he got to the end of the steel, Jamie could see how the track was laid. First the bed was prepared by scraping away the grass and some of the topsoil with a rig pulled by a team of horses. Then wagons were wheeled in to drop a thick layer of gravel. Men levelled it off with shovels and rakes, and when they were satisfied it was even, another crew began hauling in the ties.

There was tamping and adjusting and shoveling until the foreman gave the signal that everything was level, and the crew carried the heavy steel rail into place. Fishplates had to be put between the rail and the tie, and each rail had to be bolted to the ones in front and behind. Surveyors sighted down their transits, the foreman gave a final check to see that the rails were exactly four feet eight-and-a-half inches apart, and finally the spikes were driven home.

The end of the steel was a great hive of activity. Wagons were coming and going, men carried ties and rails, workers and foremen shouted to each other, and the sounds of big hammers driving the spikes filled the air. But despite the seeming chaos, everything went like clockwork.

"If only I could work on construction," Jamie thought to himself, as he walked on to where another crew was building a bridge across the Sable River. The bridge was 150 feet long. Two wooden pillars had been sunk on either side of the river bank, and long twelve-inch square timbers joined them together. Now the men were setting the struts and supports that flared out from the pillars to carry the heavy weight of the trains.

Jamie found a spot on a grassy rise overlooking the river and sat down to rest. A kingfisher flew a few feet

1. This engraving of London's Great Western Railway station and yards was drawn in 1875. With the coming of the Great Western, the Grand Trunk and other railways in the middle of the nineteenth century, the city became a major rail centre.

2. The Great Western Railway station was London's transportation hub. Railways not only made travel for individuals faster and more comfortable, but also made the marketing of goods easier and cheaper. This brought prosperity to farmers and stimulated the growth of cities.

3. This wood-burning locomotive was used on the London, Huron and Bruce Railroad. A contemporary wrote: it "speeded through the bush at the rate of 12 to 15 miles per hour from Wingham to London."

4. The locomotive "Josephine" was used on the Canadian Northern Railway. Railroad workers kept their machines polished and immaculate. To many in the nineteenth century, the locomotive was the proud symbol of progress.

5. Railroad companies built and repaired many of their own engines and running stock. These workers, in Montreal's Pointe St. Charles Grand Trunk car works, are building a wood-burning locomotive.

6. The London Car Works was opened in 1874. The skilled craftsmen in these shops had the talent to resurrect a freight car wrecked in a derailment or to remodel stylishly a passenger coach.

7. In 1882 the Great Western merged with the Grand Trunk, making it one of the largest railway companies in the world. The London Car Works was responsible for the repair and upkeep of the company's rolling stock over a large area of southwestern Ontario.

8. When railway lines were under construction they employed a large number of unskilled labourers. This is a photo of a road-building crew but railroad construction workers used similar equipment. The top soil was scraped away with plow-like rigs pulled by teams of horses. Then a thick layer of gravel was laid down, ties were put on top and the rails laid.

9. Much construction work depended on the brute strength of the labourers. The gravel ballast was shovelled by hand, rails had to be carried by teams of men and spikes were driven home with heavy, long-handled hammers.

10. Train wrecks were common in the last century. Many were the result of poorly constructed tracks or bridges, but others were caused by human error. In this wreck the train hit a wagon at a crossing. The engineer was killed and several people were injured.

11. This is London's Richmond Street looking north from King in 1855. The city had boardwalks, dirt streets and gas lighting.

12. As prosperity increased in southwestern Ontario, cities and towns grew. People increasingly bought necessities rather than producing them at home. This store in London stocked a fine selection of hats for men and women.

13. Blacksmiths were closely connected to the carriage trade. Most smithys earned their living by shoeing horses, but they also repaired farm implements and made other iron goods. The blacksmith would heat the iron in his forge until it was red hot and became soft. He then would shape it by beating it with his hammer on an anvil.

14. Prior to the railway, stagecoaches were the most important form of overland travel. Passengers often sat up on the roof of the coach and got a good rolling because of the poor roads and hard-driving stage.

15. This is the City Hotel on the corner of Dundas and Talbot Streets in London as it looked in the 1870s. Most of the hotels were involved in the carriage trade by providing stabling and horses for the stage-coach companies. For many years the City Hotel was the London terminal of the Donnelly Stage Line that ran north up the Proof Line Road, through Lucan to Exeter.

16. The Mechanic's Institute in London was in the Court House Square on Fullerton Street. The institute housed a library and reading room open to all workers. It hosted cultural events such as musical concerts and discussions on literary and scientific issues.

17. John Campbell's Carriage Factory in London made a wide variety of vehicles. Carriages, wagons and stagecoaches were manufactured in many communities.

18. This log shack and stable is typical of the buildings put up by the first settlers in southwestern Ontario. The rotting stumps are all that remain of the original forest.

19. Horses and wagons were the basic means of transportation for farmers.

20. During the American Civil War in the 1860s many farmers and merchants in southwestern Ontario became prosperous because they were able to market their grain and cattle in the United States. Large houses, such as this one in Lucan, were built during this period and remain standing today.

21. The Atlantic Petroleum Works, on Hamilton Road in the east end of London, refined crude oil, found in the Sarnia area. Railroads were very important in the development of industries such as this because they provided a cheap way of transporting raw materials and gave manufacturers access to large markets.

over the water, hunting for food, and disappeared under the bridge. Lazily Jamie rolled over, lay on his back and watched the white puffy clouds drift overhead. He felt so tired .... Gently he slipped into sleep.

He woke with a shock. The sun had drifted across the sky, and the air was beginning to get chilly. "It's late," he muttered to himself. "Past four-thirty!"

Quickly he got to his feet and began running towards the cook tent. "Mr. Henry will be furious," he thought. But it wasn't his fault. He just wasn't cut out for kitchen work.

Jamie paused at the door to the tent and tried to collect himself. Meg was busy tending one of the stoves when he entered. She looked up at him reproachfully.

The cook shouted as soon as he saw him. "Give you a little time off and you take half a day!"

"Mr. Henry, like ... " Jamie stammered nervously. "Like I was hoping ... "

"Jamie, don't!" Meg warned.

He pressed ahead. "Like, I was hoping I could get a job with the construction crew as water boy or something like that."

"Water boy!" The cook's eyes widened. "You can't even work as a cook's help. How can you expect to work with a construction crew?"

Jamie was annoyed. "I could run messages and get them things."

"Now you listen to me," said Mr. Henry furiously. "You're fit to scrub pots and nothin' else. Understand?" The tall man bent down to the boy's level. "Cheap labour you are, and you're gonna live out your days as cheap labour. Now don't you get ideas in your head about workin' as a railroad man. In this camp either you're a cook's help, or you're nothin'."

Jamie was shaking with anger.

"I'm watchin' you, boy." Mr. Henry breathed threateningly. "I'm watchin', and if you step out of line just one more time, you're gonna be walkin' back to London all by your lonesome. Is that clear?" The cook straightened up, but a scowl was still on his face. "The two of you get back at work right quick. And I want to see some sweat on your brow."

"Yes, sir," said Meg. "Jamie, you'll work hard, won't you?" But her brother walked away in silence.

They worked non-stop to get ready for the evening meal. While Mr. Henry mixed up a batter for the dumplings in a big stoneware bowl, Meg was getting the bread ready to put on the tables, and Jamie hauled in firewood for the stoves.

At ten minutes past six, they heard the sound of the construction locomotive bringing the men back from the head of the steel. Wagonloads of workers arrived from the wreck, full of men ravenously hungry from eleven hours of heavy labour.

Mr. Henry dished up huge bowls of steaming stew with dumplings floating in it, and Meg and Jamie rushed them to the tables. The men filled their plates two and often three times. Loaves of bread were consumed, jugs of milk, cookies by the hundreds and pudding by the vat loads. When they had finally eaten enough, the workers drank tin cups of tea and filled their pipes. Then they lit their tobacco and wandered out into the warm evening to relax.

But work was not over for Jamie and Meg. They grabbed a quick bite of supper themselves and then began the long tedious job of washing and drying the mountains of dishes, cups, cutlery, pots and pans. It was after eight o'clock when they finished. When they came out of the cook tent, stars were coming out, but there was still light in the western sky, giving a mellow glow to the evening. Jamie and Meg walked down the track a hundred yards or more, absorbing the sounds, smells and sights of the dying day, but soon they turned back. The five o'clock wake-up call would come too soon.

When they got back to the boxcar where they slept, Jamie lit the candle, and they got ready for bed. After they were settled, Jamie whispered out of the darkness. "Meg, I just want you to know. I'm not going to put up with Mr. Henry much longer."

"Just try, Jamie. Please."

Meg lay on her back with thoughts crowding through her head. Jamie worried her. He had grown up a lot since they had left Ottawa a year before, but he still found it hard to put in a full day's work.

Now she could hear his steady breathing and knew he was asleep. She sighed. Sometimes the responsibility of working and looking after her brother was almost too much. If the family could only come together again her mother could share the load, and it would be nice to have someone worry about her for a change.

Meg thought hard. Two hundred dollars was a lot of money. Everyone seemed to believe that the Ryan boys had chopped down the tree. If she could get evidence linking the brothers to the train wreck, she could claim the reward. But how? She just didn't know.

CHAPTER 7

THE next afternoon Mr. Henry told Meg to go into town to buy some supplies. Jamie wanted to go as well, but the cook would not hear of it. "You've got work to do, boy."

"But it's not fair that Meg gets to go into town, and I don't."

"There's lots of things that are not fair in this world. One thing I'm learnin' is that you don't do your fair share of the work around here." Mr. Henry stood with his hands on his hips, piercing him with his sharp blue eyes.

Jamie kicked the ground angrily and began walking away. "You're a jailer," he muttered under his breath.

"What's that you say?"

"Nothing."

As Meg was harnessing up the horse, the boy came out of the cook tent to see her off. He was wearing a long white apron, and his brown hair was tousled. He looked dejected.

"Don't feel so sorry for yourself, Jamie."

"I'd like to escape from this place."

"For heaven's sake, stop complaining," Meg said impatiently as she climbed up onto the seat of the wagon. "I'll be back soon, and then maybe we can do something nice together." The girl slapped the reins across the horse's back, the wagon jerked forward, and she was off.

As the horse trotted along the road, the wheels kicked up dust. Overhead the sun glared out of a cloudless sky, baking the fields to a golden yellow. On one side was a pasture with half a dozen milking cows, and on the other was a big field of corn. The land looked prosperous with its deep, loamy soil.

She didn't have time to worry about Jamie now. She was going into town. What better place to start finding out about the Ryan brothers?

Soon the wagon road came to the London-Goderich Highway, and Meg turned south towards the church steeples of Exeter. Within minutes she had passed the outskirts of town and come into the business section.

Mr. Henry had said Graham's Grocery Store was located just past the hotel. Without slowing the pace of the horse, she turned the corner where the Ryans had met the railroaders and reined to a stop in front of the store.

Inside were big sacks of sugar and flour. Potatoes, carrots and onions were stacked neatly on the floor in bushel baskets beside quarts of peaches, apples and pears. Preserves in tidy-looking bottles lined the shelves to the ceiling, and there were strange varieties of spices and teas.

Meg waited patiently while the shopkeeper, a middle-aged man in a clean white apron, served another customer. He had long bushy sideburns that met in a moustache. His balding hair was parted in the middle and slicked down with heavily perfumed oil. As she waited, she studied notices that customers had put up on a post inside the shop. One advertised for a stable boy in the hotel.

"Yes?" the man said to Meg in a sing-song voice as the other customer left.

"I work for the railway, Mr. Graham, and was sent by the cook to get a few things."

"My, my. Even the railroad is starting to hire females. What is the world coming to?" His eyebrows arched upwards in disapproval.

Meg produced the long list Mr. Henry had prepared, and the storekeeper began filling the order.

The girl lounged nervously against the counter. Would this be the place to start asking about the Ryans? She had to start somewhere. Awkwardly she blundered ahead.

"Ah … Mr. Graham, sir. Do you know the Ryan brothers?"

The storekeeper had fixed a pair of wire glasses to the end of his nose to read the list. He looked at Meg over the top of them. "The Ryan brothers … ?"

"The ones who run the London-Exeter stage."

"Why do you ask?"

Meg fiddled with a piece of paper on the counter. "Just … like … what do you think of them?"

"They're stagecoach men. What more can I say?" His face showed his disdain, and then he went back to filling her order.

She waited a moment and then pressed on. "Do they cause any trouble?"

"Trouble? Why do you ask that?"

"No ... no real reason, sir. I was just wondering, like ... ." She wanted to merge into the woodwork.

"Hmmm." The shopkeeper gathered a whole armload of things, brought them over to the counter and set them down carefully. Then he leaned forward until he was so close to Meg that she found the smell of the perfumed oil in his hair overpowering. "I make it a policy never to talk about my customers."

"It's just that, like, I'm from the railway, you see, sir, and ... and some railroaders think that the Ryans caused a wreck on the line." As soon as she said it, Meg feared she had told him too much.

"I heard about that," Mr. Graham said simply, regarding the girl over his glasses. "But I wouldn't like to speculate on who was responsible." He folded his arms across his apron and looked at her without smiling.

Meg realized she was getting nowhere. "Is there anyone around who could tell me something about it?"

"You might try the blacksmith."

"The blacksmith?" She looked out the window to the shop across the street.

"He's friendly with the Ryan boys."

"Really? Thanks. I will."

"You go ahead," Mr. Graham said smoothly. "I'll just make up the bill and put the things into your wagon. After you're finished, you can get the ice from the shed in back."

Across the dusty street was a large shop with a big open door. Overhead a weather-worn sign announced: George Jones, Blacksmith. When the girl approached she could see the forge glowing red as the bellows blew the fire into life. A moment later came the ringing of the hammer as the blacksmith shaped a horseshoe on the anvil.

Meg paused at the open doorway and peered nervously inside. A heavy brown horse was tethered tightly to a rail. It moved skittishly with each ring of the hammer. The smithy was a big, solid man with massive arms and stomach. He wore a heavy leather apron over his naked chest. Around his throat was tied a red scarf.

When he had finished shaping the shoe, the blacksmith thrust it into water, where it sizzled and sent up a puff of steam. Then he carried it across to the animal in a pair of tongs, lifted up one of the horse's front legs, which he held between his knees, positioned the shoe carefully on the hoof and began nailing it in place. After he was done he dropped the horse's foot, stood up and looked at the girl standing in the doorway.

"What can I do for you?" he drawled.

"Ah, are you Mr. Jones?" Meg inquired.

"That's what they call me." The blacksmith dropped his tools on his workbench, took off his neckerchief and mopped his forehead.

Meg stepped inside. "I ... I understand you know the Ryans."

"That's the truth." He scratched himself, and the muscles on his arms rippled.

"Could you answer a few questions about them?"

The man looked at Meg curiously. "What's there to know? They're stagecoach men. Best in the country. That's how they've run every other company in these parts out of business." The big man was wiping his huge greasy hands on a cloth.

"How far would they go to ... to run a company out of business, I mean?"

"What's it to you?" Now there was suspicion in his voice.

Meg backed up nervously. "Just asking."

The man took a step towards the girl. "Who are you?"

"From ... from the railroad, sir," she stammered.

"Railroad? You're from the railroad?"

Meg took another step backwards.

"And what do you want with the Ryans? Why come snoopin' around here?"

"It's just ... "

"That railroad is up to no good. Will Ryan says it's gonna try to drive the stagecoach and blacksmiths and everyone like us out of business. Is that right, girl?"

"I don't know, sir. Really I don't."

"It better not. That's all I can say. I make my livin' keepin' horses shod in these parts, and I don't take kindly to anyone who might threaten it."

She had backed out into the street now.

The blacksmith paused for a moment and began tying his scarf around his neck again. "Why do you wanna know about the Ryans?"

"Nothing ... it's nothing."

"You tryin' to collect information for the railroad?"

"Nothing like that."

"It's like them people on the railroad to hire a young girl to ask questions."

"I didn't mean anything, sir." Suddenly she turned and fled across the street.

"The stage will drive the railway under. You'll see!" the blacksmith shouted after her. "That steam box is doomed!"

When Meg got back to the wagon she was trembling. The Ryans and their friends were everywhere in this country. She should have known better than to have asked questions of the blacksmith. Anyone who made their living off horses would want to protect the stage.

It took a few minutes to steer the wagon in behind the store and wait while the clerk of the grocery store wrestled three big blocks of ice into the back of the wagon. Meg covered them with a piece of heavy canvas and then steered the horse past the hotel's stables towards the street.

As she was coming through the alleyway between the stores, Bobby Ryan emerged from the shadows. He grabbed the horse by the bridle and brought the wagon to a sudden stop.

"Let go!" Meg screamed.

Quick as a cat, Bobby leapt up onto the wagon. He grabbed her arm roughly. "What are you doin'?" he demanded.

"I've got a right to be here."

"You've been goin' around town askin' people about us Ryans. What do you want?" Bobby was twice her size.

"Nothing."

"You're lyin'! The smitty told me about it. You're from the railway."

Meg could hear her heart beating rapidly. She didn't know what to say.

"What's going on here?" Mr. Graham demanded. The shopkeeper was standing on the boardwalk out in front of his store with his hands on his hips. Two farm women had stopped in the street to listen to the argument. Others were gathering.

For a moment Bobby seemed uncertain what to do. He turned on Meg, squeezing her arm painfully. "You be careful, 'cause we're watchin' you!" Then he jumped to the ground, strode across to a bay horse that was tethered close by, leapt on its back and galloped south out of town.

"Are you all right?" the shopkeeper asked.

"Why did he do that?" Meg was shaken.

"Some say the Ryan boys are heroes. Others think they're outlaws. There's those that blame everything on them: barn burnings, animals mutilated, shootings. But I've seen Will Ryan playing his fiddle at a barn bee, and you would have thought he was a friend of every man in the township." The shopkeeper shook his head slowly. "One thing for sure. You don't mess with them lightly."

CHAPTER 8

THE horse clomped along the track leading back to the camp, kicking up grasshoppers and crickets with the dust. Goldfinches swooped in to catch the juicy bugs, and groundhogs scurried for their burrows to get away from the heavy hooves.

"Bunch of bullies," Meg muttered to herself. Her fear had turned into a cold anger.

As she steered in behind the cook tent, Jamie came outside to help her. "Anything happen in town?" he asked as he tied the horse to the hitching post. He was glad to get out of the kitchen.

Meg talked as she climbed to the ground. "The Ryan boys are guilty of wrecking the train. I'm sure of that now."

"How do you know? Did you get proof?"

"They did it, all right."

As they carried the provisions into the cook tent, Meg explained what had happened in Exeter. Jamie listened carefully.

"But that doesn't mean they're guilty," he said after she had finished.

"Then why did Bobby attack me?"

"Maybe he was just trying to find out what you were doing."

"They caused the wreck, and we've got to find a way to stop them before they do a lot more damage to the railway."

Jamie was leaning against the back of the wagon with his arms folded. "Maybe they're just scared or suspicious or something."

"You weren't there."

"But … "

"No good scamp! Wastin' time again." It was Mr. Henry.

Instantly the boy sprang to his feet and tried to appear busy.

The cook was standing at the door to the tent. "I tell you I've about run out of patience, boy."

"I'm just talking to my sister, sir."

"Laze around all the time. You don't know how to put in a good day's work."

"You're not fair. I work as hard as anyone else."

"You always want to be outside and work with the navvies, or ride the trains, or go into town. You won't buckle down and do an honest day's work in my kitchen. That's what we pay you for."

"That's not true, Mr. Henry. You watch what I do every minute and won't give me a moment's rest."

"That's right, and I'm going to continue watching until you shape up." The cook stomped away and left the two of them to carry in the groceries.

"I can't stand him, Meg." The boy rubbed the tired ache in the back of his neck. "He won't leave me alone."

"You've got to try harder, Jamie."

"I am trying. You nag me just like him!"

"We've got to keep these jobs. It's all we've got."

"I don't care about this stupid job. I want to get something else."

"But there are no other jobs. We looked everywhere. Remember? We've got to work so we can send money back home."

The boy didn't have the strength to argue anymore. He felt incredibly tired, as if all of his inner reserve had drained out of him. The twelve- to fourteen-hour work days were taking their toll.

They unloaded the groceries from the wagon and then found a couple of men to put the heavy blocks of ice in the shed the camp used as a cooler. Afterwards they went back to the kitchen to help get ready for supper.

Mr. Henry moodily watched Jamie like a hawk. Often the boy would glance up and notice the cook's eyes on him.

At six in the evening the big triangle bell was rung, marking the end of the working day. Hungry men streamed into the cook tent. Jamie and Meg were set running to bring the big pans of shepherd's pie, steaming bowls of potatoes and mounds of turnips. The labourers' appetites seemed impossible to satisfy.

The crew had been settled for no more than a couple of minutes when there was a long blast of a steam whistle. Jamie had just brought a loaf of bread to one of the tables close to the entrance of the tent, and he stuck his head outside to see what was happening.

Sam Bolt was just arriving from London in a locomotive hauling a trainload of construction materials. As the boy watched, the crew swung out of the engine, and Con Lucas, along with Mr. Mason, climbed out of the caboose. They started walking towards the cook tent.

"Get back to work," Jamie heard Mr. Henry snarl. Then the cook went outside to meet the superintendent.

A special table had to be set up for the trainmen. They only started eating when most of the other men had finished. Meg and Jamie got their own meal and went to sit at a table beside the others where they were able to hear the conversation.

"There were sheep on the tracks," Sam was explaining. "That's why we were late. Somebody ripped down a section of new fence and this whole herd of them were out on the track. Took us the best part of an hour to round them up, get 'em back into the farmer's field and repair the fence."

"This is the second time in three days that there has been an incident on the line," said Mason, the superintendent.

"How did the fence get torn down?" someone asked.

"Unless I miss my guess, it was them Ryan boys again." The big engineer was tucking into a huge helping of shepherd's pie.

Mason stirred his tea thoughtfully while the others sat around looking glum. "Wrecks are expensive. If there's any more damage, the company could close down the line. We've got to find a way to stop it."

"What can we do?" asked Sam.

"I'm going to order a speed limit of fifteen miles per hour until this thing is solved, and there will be no running on the track at night. But that's just temporary. We have to catch those who are responsible."

"But how?"

"I don't know. Maybe we'll print up posters announcing the two hundred dollar reward and put them on every tree and fencepost in the township. The railway would be happy to pay the money if it would flush out the culprits."

Mr. Henry wouldn't let Meg and Jamie listen to any more of the discussion. "All right, you two. There's plenty of dishes waitin' for you. Get a move on."

The chores after the evening meal were the hardest part of the day for Meg and Jamie. They were both tired, but stacks of dishes from two hundred men had to be washed before they were finished for the night.

The water had been left on the stove to heat while the crew was eating supper. Meg began the tedious task of scraping all of the leftovers into a garbage pail while Jamie set out the big corrugated-iron wash tub on the table, poured in powdered soap and then added the hot water.

The boy put on his apron, dumped in a stack of dishes and cups and began washing. Soon Meg and Jamie were the only ones left in the big white cook tent. It began to get dark. They lit coal-oil lanterns and hung them on the poles that held up the tent.

The heat from the water and the long hours of work made the boy tired. All he wanted to do was climb into bed and sleep the night away, but he forced himself to wash the dishes, one after the other. No matter how much he worked, they never seemed to get to the end of the huge stacks.

"I've just got to take a rest, Meg," he said finally.

"Are you all right?"

He collapsed onto one of the benches, put his arms on the table and rested his head. He felt dizzy. He had been working since five that morning without a break. There was not a part of his body that did not ache.

As he sat on the bench resting his head on the table, the dull ache that spread from his neck down to the small of his back slowly began to ease. He was drifting off to sleep.

"Jamie!! Jamie Bains!! What are you doing?"

The boy sprang to his feet, confused and disoriented. "I ... what ... ?"

It was Mr. Henry, and he was flaming mad. "I leave you for a few minutes, and when I'm gone you go to sleep. Well, I've had it from you, boy!"

"He's tired, Mr. Henry," Meg explained weakly.

"After tonight he can get lots of rest, because he's not going to be working for me."

Jamie could feel tears gathering in his eyes. "You just don't like me. That's all. You never liked me, Mr. Henry."

"It has nothing to do about likes or dislikes. I want someone who's going to work."

"I work as hard as anyone else." Tears were rolling down the boy's face.

"You avoid work every chance you get."

"It's not true. You're not fair. I've been working all day. Even Meg got a chance to rest when she went into town."

"He's just tired, Mr. Henry," Meg said. "Once he's had a good night's sleep, he'll be better."

"He's not going to work for me again. He's finished for good."

Jamie was taking off his apron. He bundled it up and threw it on the table. "Well, I don't want to work here anyway!" he screamed. "You're a tyrant. We work harder than the construction workers, get paid almost nothing, and … "

"I don't want you around my camp any longer, boy! Now get out of my cook tent and don't come back!"

Jamie wiped the tears wetting his cheeks. He looked at Meg and back at the tall cook. Then he stalked out of the tent.

It was a good half hour or more before Meg finished the dishes and could get away. She found her brother sitting on the steps that led up to their sleeping quarters. He looked so forlorn that she felt close to tears herself.

"He wasn't fair, Meg. I worked as hard as anyone in the camp."

"I'm going to ask Mr. Mason if he'll speak to Mr. Henry and make him take you back," she said.

He looked up at his sister. "I'll never work for him again! I'd starve first! I'm going to get a job on construction, or something like that."

"But what about Mother? She's counting on us."

"I'm not staying here anymore!"

Now Meg was annoyed. "You're just thinking of yourself, Jamie. Don't be so selfish."

"I'm not selfish. Tomorrow I'm going into Exeter. I'll take the stage into London to look for another job." There was a stubborn edge to the boy's voice.

"We can't split up! Who would look after you, Jamie?"

"You never helped me with Mr. Henry. I'm almost thirteen now. I can look after myself. No one's going to catch me in this stinking camp again!"

CHAPTER 9

JAMIE got up with Meg at five the next morning and began getting his gear together. He had a lot of ground to cover if he was going to catch the seven o'clock stage.

Meg sat on the bed and watched her brother. "Jamie, this isn't right. We shouldn't split up like this. What would Mother say?"

"I don't want anything more to do with this stupid railway."

"But we've been together so long now, and we've had tough times before. Remember Toronto? The problem is that you've got so independent that you won't listen to me."

"Not if all you do is give me another lecture on what a bad worker I am."

Meg started to cry. "I hate this life, too, Jamie. It seems like we never get any closer to getting the family together." She wiped her tears with the back of her hand. "If only Mother was here. I miss her and the kids so much. Now you're going away."

The boy stood at the door, holding his canvas sack and watching his sister. He felt close to tears himself.

"Let me talk to Mr. Mason. Please!" she pleaded.

"I can't stay."

Meg sighed. She stood up and began searching in the deep pocket of her dress. Carefully she extracted the last of their money. Seventy-seven cents — three quarters and two big pennies. "It's all we've got left," she said, handing it to him.

The boy looked up at his sister. "But what about you, Meg?"

"I've got wages coming from the railroad, and at least I'll get fed and have a place to sleep."

"I can look after myself."

"Take it. But, Jamie, you've got to promise me that you'll let me know where you are. If I don't hear from you I'll be sick with … "

"Don't worry about me! I can look after myself."

Meg smiled. "Give me five minutes and come to the back door of the cook tent." Then she was gone.

Jamie gathered up the rest of his things, felt the seventy-seven cents in his pocket, took one last look around the tiny sleeping cubicle and left.

His sister was waiting for him with a small sack. "It's food. Enough to get you through the day. After that … "

The boy smiled. For so long Meg had thought of things for the two of them. When he had got into trouble, she had been the one who looked after him. Now he would be on his own.

"Thanks, Meg," he whispered.

Tears were gathering in her eyes as she gave her brother a hug. "Just let me know where you are. And if you change your mind, come back and I'll talk to Mr. Mason."

"Goodbye, Meg." The boy slung the sacks over his shoulder and headed to the wagon trail.

As he walked down the road towards the highway, the red ball of the sun broke the horizon in front of him. It was very quiet. Heavy dew, clinging to the grass and trees, gleamed in the early-morning sunshine. Overhead the pale sky darkened to a deep blue as the sun rose.

The boy took an apple out of the sack that Meg had given him and ate it as he walked along. Once he got to the highway and turned south towards the town, he began to lengthen his stride. He would have to hurry if he was to catch the seven o'clock stage.

As he came down the main street of town, he could see the stage loading out in front of the Exeter Hotel. Passengers were milling around on the porch, someone was up on top of the coach lashing down trunks, carpet bags and valises, while Will Ryan stood, whip in hand, taking money from a thin, middle-aged man wearing a clergyman's collar. The driver glanced up and smiled at the young boy without recognizing him.

"Can I help you?" he asked.

Jamie smiled. "Could I get a ticket to London on the stage?"

"Cost you a dollar."

"A dollar. I ... I haven't got that much."

"Can't take people for free."

"But ... "

"Could wait to ride down on the railroad, but it might be a long time before she ever gets finished," Will laughed good naturedly.

"I've had enough of working for the railway. I've got to get to London to find a job."

"Seventy-five cents if you want to ride up on top."

"Well … " The boy hesitated.

"All right, then I'll give 'er to you for fifty cents, but don't be speakin' about it, or people will start to think the Ryans are soft." Will laughed again, showing a set of strong white teeth.

Jamie dug in his pocket and pulled out two quarters. He handed them to the stagecoach driver.

"Hope you can hold on, boy, 'cause you're in for a real rollin'."

Suddenly a figure leapt from the top of the stage onto the ground just behind them. It was Bobby Ryan, and he was looking at Jamie suspiciously. "You say you worked for the railway?"

The boy felt a sudden panic. "Well, yeah, like I did, but I quit."

Bobby's face was set. "I remember now. You were in London with the railroaders the other day, and you came into Exeter that night."

"I don't have anything to do with them anymore. I …"

"I bet you were sent to spy on us just like that girl who was snoopin' around town yesterday."

Will Ryan pushed his broad-brimmed hat to the back of his head. "Now I remember."

"He's a spy, Will."

"Is that right? Are you here to spy on us, boy?"

"No … like I told you. I just want to ride into London and get a job."

"Don't let him on the stage," whispered Bobby.

Slowly a smile came across Will's face. "The boy paid his money, so he gets his ride. Maybe he can teach us somethin' about the railway."

"But … "

"You afraid of a young boy like this, Bobby?"

"Course not. It's just that … "

The driver had pulled out his gold pocket watch, studied it for a moment and then turned to the people milling about on the hotel porch. "Climb aboard now, folks. She's almost seven, and the Ryan stage runs on time." He opened the small door of the cramped passenger compartment. A woman in a fancy hooped dress entered first, followed by the minister and three other men.

"Don't just stand there, boy," Will barked at Jamie. "Get your gear stowed and climb aboard."

Jamie lifted the heavy leather flap at the back of the stage and stuffed his canvas bags inside.

"All aboard," the driver called out in a loud voice. "Ryan stage headin' for London. Any other passengers?"

Bobby had gone to the head of the team and unhitched them. In a bound Will was aboard, gathering the reins in his hands.

Jamie was halfway up, his foot still on the wheel spoke, when suddenly, with the driver's call of "High up!" Bobby let go. Will cracked his whip over the horses' heads. With a jerk they were off.

As the wheel turned, Jamie's foot went out from under him. He clutched desperately to a handle, his legs thrashing about in the air until he found a foothold. It took all the strength in his arms to scramble up to the seat with the coach bouncing wildly under him.

Again Will cracked his whip, forcing the horses into a gallop. "On the Ryan stage you'd best hold on, boy, or all your bones will shake loose."

They thundered out of town with the horses in a hard gallop, and the coach pitching wildly as it dipped into the ruts and hollows of the dusty road. It was all Jamie could do to hold on to the hard wooden seat that was his perch.

At a cross street a farmer started a wagon in front of the stage. Will didn't pause. Recklessly he veered his team in front of the wagon, forcing the other driver to rein in to avoid a collision. Then, with one easy movement, he slapped the reins across the horses' backs and cracked his whip. They raced even faster.

Once out on the London-Goderich Road, the horses settled into a loping gallop. As they passed, cattle raised their heads, birds flew up in fright, and dogs came running out to bark at the hooves of the horses and bite at the wheels of the hard-driving stage.

"Why are you ridin' on my stage, boy?" Will shouted above the noise.

"I ... I was workin' with the railway as a cook's help, but I couldn't stand it anymore."

"That's women's work."

"That's what I thought," Jamie nodded.

Will curled back his arm and cracked the long whip over the heads of his horses. The frightened team raced down the road in full gallop.

As they rushed south, they passed inns at the corners of many of the concession roads. There were a few log buildings about, remnants of the days when the land had been cleared thirty years before, but most houses were built of white brick. They were big two- and three-storey homes with pretty gingerbread woodwork under the eaves and porches that stretched around two of the sides. The barns were big square wooden affairs weathering into a solid-looking grey colour.

At Clandeboye, a few miles south, the road turned due east. A mile or more past the bend they came to the Ausable River, which cut deeply into the flat plain. Will reined the horses to a walk to take them along the road that twisted down to the valley floor. At the bottom the stage bounced up onto the narrow wooden bridge. Again the whip cracked as Will tried to get the animals into a gallop so they would have some speed to take the hill on the other side. Despite his curses the horses soon slowed. They walked up the hill with their sides heaving.

By the time they got to the top, the animals were played out, but the driver would not let them rest. He whipped them back into a gallop again, and two miles later they approached Lucan, the home town of the Ryan boys.

The horses raced along the tree-lined street. Dogs barked, children ran out of houses waving, and merchants came to the doors of their shops to watch. Jamie felt a thrill to be at the centre of such a great commotion.

At the Revere House, a hotel on the corner of Main and Alice streets, Will finally reined his exhausted team to a halt.

"Lucan," he announced as the passengers climbed out of the coach. "The stage will leave in fifteen minutes."

Two of the people were getting off here. Jamie helped them get their bags down, and then Will wheeled the stage around to the back of the building so the horses could be changed.

As they came to a halt, the two animals stood panting heavily, their flanks lathered in sweat and caked in dust. A boy grabbed them by their halters and began unshackling them from their traces while a man led a fresh team out from the stable.

Will strode quickly across the yard to the back of the hotel. Jamie climbed down and hesitantly followed him inside. The driver was in the darkened saloon bar, nervously tapping his big brown boots with the whip. A small shot glass filled with amber-coloured liquid stood in front of him.

Will watched Jamie come up to the bar beside him. "Whatcha think of the ride, boy?"

"The stage gives quite a rolling."

"Suppose you prefer to ride in a train."

"I'd rather ride in a stage any day of the week."

"Then you're a man after my own heart, there, boy." Will slapped him on the back good-naturedly, and Jamie swelled with pride.

"You'd best get rid of the dust in your throat." The driver waved to the barman. "Give us a lemonade here."

The man looked at Jamie. "We can't serve young people."

Will's anger flared. "I say I want a lemonade, and I want it now!"

It took only a moment for the drink to appear. Jamie sipped the sweet, tart liquid greedily.

"I hear them railway men don't like us Ryans much."

"They think you dropped the tree onto their track and caused the accident."

Will laughed. "Some people would believe anythin' of us."

It gave Jamie a good feeling to be treated like an equal. "They think you're afraid that the railway will drive all the stages out of business."

The man pushed his hat to the back of his head. "The stage is the best transport there is in this country. That's the way it's always been and always will be. I'll bet every cent I have that my stage could beat that old steaming rust-box. The truth is that Sam Bolt is afraid to race me. You were there when I tried to set the wager, and you saw him back down."

"Why is it so important?" Jamie asked.

"If I can show everybody just how fast the stage is, it'll end all this talk about the railway drivin' us to bankruptcy." Will paused for a moment and stretched. "Anyway, they've been having such trouble with accidents and things, they might never survive."

"They have their problems, all right."

Will looked thoughtful for a moment. "Now drink up there, boy. We've got a stage to drive." He quickly strode out of the saloon bar with his big boots clomping on the floor.

By the time Jamie got outside, the driver was already climbing up to the box. Once he had gathered up the reins, the stable boy let go of the horses, and Will steered them around in a tight turn to drive out of the yard.

There were a number of new passengers for the run into London. They crammed inside the coach, Jamie climbed up onto the top, and with another "High up" and a crack of the whip, the stage lurched onto the road again. The fresh horses galloped out of town, leaving a big cloud of dust behind.

In a few minutes they had passed the Catholic church at the corner of the Roman Line, swept through the village of Elginfield, paid a fare at a toll booth, and were on the Proof Line Road heading due south into London. After they passed a big brick yard, the horses slowed as they climbed a long hill.

"Think my rig can beat a train in a race?" Will asked abruptly.

"Your stage is pretty fast."

"I'd like to show that big red-faced engineer he ain't as good as he thinks."

The two of them watched the horses labour up the hill. Already sweat was glistening on their sides. The sun beat down relentlessly. Jamie shed his jacket and tried to brush off some of the dust.

"Did you cause that wreck on the railway the other night?" the boy suddenly asked.

Will scowled for a moment and then smiled. "If you was to believe everythin' you hear about the Ryans, you'd think we're responsible for every crime and fire in the district."

They were nearing the top of the hill. As the grade levelled out, Will cracked his whip over the heads of his horses, and they began to pick up the pace until they were into a gallop again.

The road cut as straight as a surveyor's line over rolling hills and valleys. As the stage came into the town of Birr, Will reined his horses to a trot. He reached into a leather pouch beside him and drew out a small bundle of mail. When they were going past the post office attached to McIntosh's Hotel, he threw the package at the door. Then the whip cracked, and they were on the road again.

"Like to work around horses?" Will asked unexpectedly.

"Horses? I ... sure I would."

"If you want a job as a stable boy I might be able to help you," he announced in an off-hand way.

"Really?" Jamie was shocked at his sudden good luck.

The driver paused for a moment. "It seems that Mr. Gage in the hotel back in Exeter needs a stable boy. I could talk to him for you."

"Thanks ... thanks very much. I really need the job. Stable boy would be just perfect." He could hardly believe it.

As they rushed south along the Proof Line Road they passed hotels and saloons at the corner of every concession road. They overtook slowly lumbering wagons filled with produce on their way to market in London, buckboards carrying people, and an occasional horseback rider or a person on foot. In spite of the traffic, Will Ryan rarely slowed the pace of his team.

At the outskirts to London they had to pay another toll, and then they raced along Richmond Street with no heed to the fact that they were in a busy, built-up area. They passed prosperous homes, churches, schools and a big Protestant orphanage. After Oxford Street they went by a tannery, livery stables and shops.

Finally, at Dundas Street, Will turned west. A block later they reined up in front of the City Hotel at the corner of Talbot. They had arrived.

CHAPTER 10

"ALL right, boy, give us a hand here," Will Ryan said loudly. "If you want to be a horseman, you've got to be prepared to work."

Jamie leapt to the ground and got the luggage out of the compartment at the back of the stage, while Will helped the passengers climb from the cramped cab. Then Will took the reins and led the horses around to a small courtyard at the back of the hotel. He parked the stage and began unshackling the animals from their traces.

"Keep a close eye here, Jamie. Horses are a life's study, and you've gotta work at it if you're to be good with the beasts."

Will was a big man with strong hands and an easy confidence that the horses seemed to sense. As he worked, he talked to the boy, explaining every detail.

"Animals like this are a lot like people. They can be moody or high spirited or sick. You've gotta get to know their characters, the likes and dislikes of each one of 'em, so you can make 'em work for you and not against you."

As he talked, Will took the shafts from the heavy leather collar, unbuckled various harness straps, led the animals out of their traces and walked them across the yard to a hitching post. Sweat gleamed on their flanks and backs from the hard run, and dust and dirt clung to their bellies and legs.

"Remember that the horses are studyin' you just the same as you study them," Will continued. "You have to let them get to know you and respect you, or they'll give you nothin' but trouble. Come on, now, boy. Give me a hand getting off these collars."

Will had already grasped the heavy leather collar of one of the animals and easily lifted it over his head. Cautiously Jamie came up to the other and put a hand on the heavy, sweat-soaked fitting. Suddenly the horse bared his long yellow teeth, whinnied and tossed his head. Jamie backed away in panic.

"Don't be afraid," said Will. "Talk to him, and act like you know what you're doing. Let him smell you."

Slowly Jamie approached the huge animal again. "Come on, horse. Let me do it now, please. I'm your friend."

Again the animal snorted in fear and took a step backwards. Jamie let him sniff his arms and shoulder and then patted him on the neck while he kept up a chatter. The horse calmed, and the boy became more confident. Firmly he grasped the collar and lifted it over the animal's head.

"That's it." Will smiled. "I can see you're a born horseman." Jamie beamed proudly.

They finished taking off the harnesses and carried them into the stable. Then they went back out to the yard again and sat on a bench in the warm sun.

"It's best to let a horse cool down after a hard run," Will explained. "In a half hour or so you can rub 'em down and then we'll give 'em water and feed."

"Isn't a run like that hard on them?"

"The worse thing you can do to horses is keep them idle. A good hard gallop with the whip crackin' over their heads keeps 'em in top form." Will had stuffed a chaw of tobacco in his cheek, and he chewed on it as he talked.

"I'd like to thank you for helpin' me get a job," Jamie said as he relaxed.

"Us Ryans always help our friends. But then, I can see you'll be a good horseman, so you'll do credit. Look at them horses there, boy. They're perfect. It's taken hundreds of years of breedin' and trainin'. See the big chest and shoulders — that long, strong neck. They've got the strength of a work horse and the speed of a thoroughbred." He paused for a moment and spit a stream of brown tobacco juice onto the ground.

"Them horses helped us open this here country. They're fitted to it like a fish to water. No railroad puffin' smoke and steam is gonna change that."

"But the railroad's spreading everywhere, Will. I've seen it myself." The boy put his hands behind his head and leaned back against the stable wall. "They're laying track all over the continents. There's a line from here to Halifax in the Maritimes, and I heard they are even thinking about laying track through Canada to the West Coast."

"What good's a train if it can't move off them steel rails and go cross country? Useless. That's what I think.

Gimme a horse any day. Least it's muscle and bone. No machine is ever gonna be as smart and as strong and as loyal as a good piece of horse flesh." He spit his tobacco juice into the dust again.

"Let me tell you about this race now, boy," he continued. "She'll be a close one, I'd have to give you that, but us Ryans have got the fastest set of horses in this here country." He smiled, the wad of tobacco bulging in his cheek. "We'd be in Exeter before that old rust-bucket would be clear of London."

"It sure would be good to see." Jamie savoured the thought.

Will got to his feet. "All right, now, time's a movin'. Let's get them animals looked after."

Will got a couple of cloths, and the two of them set to work giving the horses a good rub-down. After they were finished, he led them one at a time into stalls and fed and watered them.

Jamie liked the stagecoach driver. Despite his gruff manner, he was gentle and friendly. He spent time explaining how to handle the horses, what they liked and disliked, how much grain and hay to feed them, when they needed to be rubbed down and blanketed, and how much they could be driven in a day. The boy listened carefully. He had been around horses all his life, but this was the first time anyone had made the effort to explain how to handle them. Will knew everything about horses. Even more than Meg.

Once the animals were stabled, Will went into the hotel to check on business with the clerk. Afterwards he went out to eat, while Jamie went back to sit on the bench in the sun and eat the lunch Meg had packed for him.

The boy liked the sweet, grainy smell that drifted out of the stables. When he had finished eating he went inside to look at the big horses in their stalls. A job of stable boy would be all right, he thought. What could be more important and useful than being a horseman?

As the two o'clock departure time approached, Will left the game of billiards he was playing in the hotel and headed out to the stable. Jamie helped him harness the team of horses for the trip back to Exeter. The boy led the team and coach out to the front of the hotel and stored the luggage while Will sold tickets to the passengers. Finally they were off.

The trip north was as harrowing as the one that morning. Will drove his animals relentlessly. Whenever they fell below the pace of a gallop, the whip stung the air, and the horses raced even faster.

Out on the open road Will asked Jamie to take the reins. The boy had never done anything like this before, but Will insisted, and he couldn't refuse. Carefully he gathered the leather straps in each hand and listened while the driver explained how to handle them.

"You've got to keep 'er a little slack, but always let 'em know that you're in control. Remember that those reins go down to bits in the horses' mouths. They can feel every time you move."

At first Jamie held on grimly, afraid that he might hurt the horses or steer them into the ditch. They seemed to know that someone strange was driving them, and they began to slow.

Suddenly Will cracked his whip over their heads, and with a surge of power they picked up the pace. For a moment the boy thought he was going to lose control, but then he felt the horses respond to him. He found himself moving with their rhythm.

He laughed. "I can really drive them, Will!"

"You're a horseman, boy. That's the truth. Soon you'll get the feel of her and be able to handle the reins and use the whip all at the same time."

"I'm a real horseman!" Jamie felt like shouting out of sheer pleasure.

"Don't get too confident. She takes a lifetime to learn how to handle beasts like this. The railroad think they can eliminate all of that in the half a year it takes to lay track."

A few minutes later Will took over the reins again. They went up the Proof Line Road, dropping mail and passengers, and stopping to switch horses. Finally, at about five in the evening, they got to Exeter. The stage pulled up in front of the hotel and discharged the rest of the passengers.

"Take the horses to the stable," Will shouted as he went up onto the porch of the hotel. "I'll see if Mr. Gage is around."

Jamie coiled the reins up in his hand, leaving a little slack, and began to lead the horses around the corner into the alley between the hotel and Mr. Graham's store. There he found a big stable with a courtyard. He followed the routine Will had used in London by parking the coach in an out-of-the-way spot before he began to take off the harnesses.

It was more difficult than it looked. There seemed to be buckles and straps everywhere. Finally, when the horses were free, he led them over to a hitching post and tied them up so they could cool off.

Just as he was finishing, Will came out the back door of the hotel with a small, stout man wearing a brown tweed suit and waistcoat. He had short hair with a shaggy moustache and sideburns.

"This is Jamie Bains," Will announced as he came up. "And this here is Mr. Gage."

The hotelkeeper pulled back his suit jacket and put his thumbs into his waistcoat pockets. He regarded the boy critically. "He seems rather skinny and weak to me," he said in an English accent.

"May be small, but he's a good worker. I can vouch for that."

"I dearly hope that he's better than that dreadful brother of yours."

"Aye, well, you know Bobby."

"Unfortunately I learned. I have never seen a stable left in such a mess."

"Bobby's always searchin' the countryside for adventure."

Mr. Gage examined Jamie again. "What makes you think you can do this work, lad?"

"I've worked hard all my life," Jamie said cautiously. "And I like horses."

"Know anything about the beasts?"

He glanced at Will. "A little, sir, and I can learn."

"Like I said, Mr. Gage. I'll help the boy," Will added. "He'll work out fine. You'll see."

"I must say this is against my better judgement. But you're a man of your word, Will. If you speak for the boy, it's good enough for me."

Jamie smiled broadly. "Thanks very much, sir. I won't disappoint you."

"Wages are twenty-five cents a day. You can eat all of your meals in the kitchen of the hotel and sleep in the loft above the stable. I want that place cleaned up until it's sparkling. It's a national disgrace unworthy of a British colony."

"Didn't think Canada was a colony anymore," said Will with a half smile on his face.

"You Irish never seem to learn. Queen Victoria will not allow the Empire to die."

Jamie wasn't sure what they were talking about. "Thanks very much for the job, sir. I'll keep the stables as clean as a whistle. You'll see."

"Get on with it, then." The innkeeper walked back to the hotel and disappeared inside.

When Will swung open the big doors the rank stink of manure and mouldy hay wafted outside.

"Bobby hasn't mucked out the stalls for weeks as far as I can tell," said Will. "You've got your work cut out for you." Briefly Will showed the boy around before going into the hotel to get a drink.

When he was alone, Jamie puttered about the stable. It was a mess. The dung stood six inches deep in the stalls.

The water in the rain barrel near the door had thick scum on the top. Harnesses were piled on the floor, their leather cracked and dry.

The four horses in the stalls were dirty and moved around nervously every time he came close. Jamie went up to each of them, talking in a low voice, and let them smell him all over so they would get to know him. Then he set to work giving each of them water and a portion of grain and hay.

In spite of the terrible shape of the stable, Jamie was not discouraged. Not only did he have a job, but he had got it without any help from Meg. Better still, he would be working by himself, without anyone like Mr. Henry breathing down his neck.

After he had finished, Jamie went into the kitchen of the hotel to ask if there was a place where he could dump the manure. The cook, a heavy-set, middle-aged woman by the name of Mrs. Palmer, welcomed him like he was a lost son and insisted that he sit down and have his supper.

It was wonderful. The meal was thick slices of roast pork, potatoes swimming in brown gravy, and boiled carrots. He washed it down with big glasses of creamy milk. As Jamie ate his fill the cook bent his ear with a dozen stories about Exeter, Mr. Gage and the rumours about the Ryan brothers. He was so full he could barely finish the big wedge of apple pie she gave him.

After he was done, Jamie got directions to Mr. Gage's garden, where he could take the manure by wheelbarrow. Then he headed back to the stable. As he went in, he almost ran into the haunches of a horse with a saddle on its back.

"What's goin' on here?" demanded Bobby Ryan.

Jamie was unnerved. "I … I'm the new stable boy."

"Ain't you the one from the railroad that I seen this mornin'?"

"Yes, but … " His words trailed off.

Bobby was only a couple of feet away from him now. His eyes narrowed, and his breath came heavily. "Bet you was sent here to spy on us. That right?"

"No, I … I lost my job with the railroad, and your brother told me about this and … "

"I don't believe that!" Quick as a cat, Bobby grabbed him by the wrist. He squeezed it painfully.

"You're hurting me."

"I mean to hurt you, boy." Bobby was a head taller and far stronger than Jamie. His eyes bugged out. "Tell me the truth now! You were sent here to spy on us! Weren't you?"

"No … I … "

"What's going on here?" Will Ryan was standing in the doorway of the stable.

For a moment Bobby was confused. "This here boy's from the railway."

"Let him go!"

"He's been sent to spy on us, Will!"

"I said, let him go, or you'll answer to me!"

The two brothers glared at each other. Then Bobby pushed Jamie hard. The boy stumbled and fell. He sat on the ground rubbing his wrist.

"If you ever do that again," Will said, his voice grim, "you'll get a taste of my horse whip. Understand?"

For the longest time Bobby stared at his brother. Then he stomped past him and disappeared.

CHAPTER 11

THAT evening Jamie worked for hours mucking out the stalls and wheeling the manure a block away to Mr. Gage's garden. Then he washed down the floor of the stable and spread a thick layer of fresh straw in the stalls.

By the time he was finished it was dark, and he was exhausted. He found an old blanket and, taking the lantern, he climbed up into the loft, made a nest for himself in the hay, blew out the light and fell asleep with his clothes on.

"Jamie! Jamie!" It was Will Ryan. He had thrown open the big doors, and early-morning light was streaming into the darkened stable.

The boy hurried down the ladder. They had to get the horses and stage ready for the run to London.

"What a change to this place," Will was saying. He had pushed his hat to the back of his head and was smiling. "She smells as sweet as a clover field."

The boy was pleased. "Well, I made a beginning."

"Work must be your middle name, there, Jamie boy."

Will led the horses out of their stalls and into the courtyard while Jamie got the collars and harnesses. First the stage driver put on the halters and the bits into the horses' mouths. Then he fit the collars over their heads and began buckling the straps and fitting the shafts into place.

"Gonna have to do somethin' about these here harnesses," he said. "The leather's all dried out and cracked. Every couple of days you have to rub 'em down with saddle soap."

"I'll start on it today."

When they were finished, the boy began to lead the animals through the alley to the front of the hotel. Will talked as he walked beside him.

"Those other horses in the stable need to be exercised or they're going to be good for nothin' Why don't you saddle 'em up and take 'em for a ride?"

"Are you sure that'd be all right?"

"That's your job, boy. You'll find an old saddle in the stable somewhere."

Jamie watched the stage disappear down the street before he walked around to the back of the hotel. The delicious smell wafting out of the kitchen reminded him how hungry he was. When he went inside, Mrs. Palmer cooked him up a country-sized serving of eggs, ham and fried potatoes. "A breakfast that'll get you set for a good day's work," as she put it.

When he headed back to the stable it occurred to him that maybe he could exercise one of the horses by riding out to the railway construction camp, but he wasn't sure if he should take the chance. After all, he had told Will that he had cut off his connection with the railway.

Jamie really wanted to go out to the camp. He had promised Meg that he would keep in touch with her, but that wasn't the real reason. He wanted to show Mr. Henry and all the others that he had been able to get a job by himself. At least someone thought he was a good worker. It would be worth going to the camp just to see their faces when he told them he had a job as a stable boy.

The boy fed the horses and looked at each of them carefully. With the exception of the one that Bobby rode, even his untrained eye could see that they were not in good shape. Will was right. Exercise was what they needed.

It was as he was sorting through the harnesses that Bobby came into the stable. He glared at the young boy for a moment and then got his reddish-brown horse out of the stall and walked him into the courtyard. A moment later he came back for his saddle and the rest of the gear. It was not long before the sound of hooves announced that he was riding away.

Jamie chose a creamy-coloured animal because he seemed quieter than the others. The boy got his things together and then took the horse outside. Gently he talked to him and tried to slip the bit into his mouth. But as soon as the big animal saw what was happening, he clamped his jaw shut. The more Jamie coaxed, the more stubborn the horse became.

The boy was about to give up when he had an idea. He got a handful of oats and held it in front of the horse's nose. The temptation was too much. As the big lips lapped up the grain, he slipped the bit between the animal's teeth.

Jamie didn't have much experience saddling horses, but he had seen it done lots of times. He pulled the cinch tight so it wouldn't slip and adjusted the stirrups. When he was finished, he led the horse to the front of the hotel. Only then did he try to mount.

At first the horse was skittish and shied away from him. But when he swung his foot over and settled into the saddle, the animal stood stiffly and refused to budge. Jamie nudged him gently in the ribs with his feet, but nothing happened.

He had to get the horse moving, but how? People had stopped to watch. Jamie tried everything from speaking into the long silky ears to mild smacks on the shoulder. Finally, out of frustration, he slapped the animal's rump with the end of the long reins. Instantly the horse reared up and began to bolt.

Faster and faster he was racing down the street out of town. The wind whipped past as the hooves hammered on the hard-packed dirt road. Jamie squeezed his knees together and pulled back on the reins, but it did no good. He was in a hard gallop, completely beyond control.

Jamie fought his panic and began to move with the motion of the big animal. He loosened the reins to give the horse his head, and the two rode together. They galloped north on the highway until the horse was wet with perspiration and his chest heaved. Only then did he slow and come to a halt.

The boy talked soothingly to the cream-coloured animal. For a moment the horse trembled all over. Then he stood quiet and docile. When they started again, the animal was responsive to every touch of the rider. Jamie began him in a walk and then moved into an easy trot. He concentrated on the horse, learning how he responded, and changed directions by moving the reins. By the time they got to the wagon road that led towards the construction camp, the horse and the boy rode easily together.

When the camp came into sight, Jamie saw that the boxcars that had been converted into sleeping compartments were hooked up to the locomotive. Crowds of men were carrying benches, chairs and tables out of the big cook tent and stacking them on flatcars. They were breaking camp.

As he rode up, the boy spotted Meg washing dishes in a big iron tub set up on a makeshift table behind the cook tent.

"Meg," he called. "Meg, it's me, Jamie!"

She looked up, brushing away a strand of hair that had fallen into her eyes. "Jamie? Is that really you?"

The boy slid from his horse as she came running to him. "I've been so worried. Look at you — a horse and everything." They were both laughing as she gave him a big hug.

"Will Ryan got me a job as a stable boy in the hotel in Exeter."

"Will Ryan?" She was shocked.

"Yeah, like. He's really nice, Meg. I got to know him going down to London on the stage."

"Will Ryan is responsible for the terrible things that have been happening on the railway."

"He said he didn't do it."

"And you believe him? He's the next thing to an outlaw."

"But that's not true, Meg."

"What are you doin' here, boy?" It was Mr. Henry. The cook was scowling.

Jamie gathered his courage. "I came to see my sister."

"Thought I told you that I didn't want you around here no more."

"I just came to tell her where I'm working."

"Who'd want to hire a layabout like you?" The cook leaned forward threateningly.

"I'm working in Exeter as a stable boy with the Ryans."

Mr. Henry paused and his eyes grew wide. "Well, I should have known. People the likes of you and the Ryans always find each other. Bunch of bandits. I'll be tellin' Mr. Mason about this."

Mr. Henry turned and stomped away to supervise the loading of his kitchen on the flatcar, leaving Meg and Jamie at the back of the tent.

"He's always the same," Jamie said angrily. "How can you stand to put up with him?"

"You'd best go, Jamie. If he comes back there'll be trouble."

"I just came to tell you about my new job. You can get in touch with me at the hotel in town. If you come in for supplies, ask for me."

"Maybe you should try to find some other work."

Jamie had already swung himself into the saddle. He looked down at his sister standing behind the washtubs. "I'm a stable boy, Meg. It's what I want to do." He turned his horse around and began heading out of camp.

It was as Jamie was riding away that he thought he spotted a figure sitting on a horse in among some trees, watching the activity around the railway camp. Somehow the horse looked familiar, but it wasn't until the man turned around that Jamie thought he recognized the face. It looked like Bobby Ryan.

Meg finished scrubbing the pots and then went to see how the work was progressing. The men had loaded all of the tables and chairs and now began to dismantle the kitchen. A group carried the three ranges, with their stove pipes still smoking, out to the flatcar. Others lugged the boxes of plates, cutlery, pots and pans, drinking mugs and huge jugs. All of the food had to be brought: potatoes, sacks of flour and sugar containers of milk, fresh baked bread, sides of beef and butchered hogs. The stuff seemed to be unending. Finally the crew took down the big tent, folded it and hauled the heavy canvas aboard one of the cars.

Through the whole move, Mr. Henry was constantly shouting orders. He stationed Meg around the food and told her to make sure that no one broke any of the dishes. When they finished loading about half of their supplies, the cook ordered the crew to jump aboard. They would pick up the rest on the next trip. With a blast of the whistle the train set off.

It was a short trip through the countryside. They went across the bridge over the Sable River, and four miles on ahead to a site beside a concession road near the end of the steel. Then the action began all over again: setting up the tent, chairs, stoves and all the rest.

They had barely begun when one of the men shouted, "Look at the smoke!"

"She's back at the old camp!" said another. "Somethin's lit. Come on!"

The crew of men jumped back on the flatcars. Sam was in the engine. He blew the whistle and the train began to roll. Meg ran to catch up. A couple of the navvies grabbed her arms and pulled her aboard. The closer they got to the camp, the more dense and black the smoke became.

Jamie was back on the highway, riding his horse in an easy trot, when he happened to turn around and saw the smoke. It was at the camp; he was sure of it.

The boy wheeled his horse around and began galloping back down the highway. It was then that he noticed Bobby Ryan riding hard across the open fields heading towards town. There could be no mistaking it now. He was riding his reddish-brown horse and wearing his dark woollen shirt and big floppy brown hat.

The smoke was a thick billowing black cloud that seemed to fill the sky. As the boy rode into the camp, he could see that a big stack of hay was on fire. On top of the stack were piled boxes and tools from the camp. The flames roared furiously, consuming everything.

Just at that moment, his horse shied from the smoke and flames. Jamie was caught off balance and was thrown from the saddle. When he hit the ground, his head struck something hard.

The train steamed through the countryside at top speed. Men were talking in excited voices, and Meg strained to see what was on fire. They went over the bridge and up a small rise. Finally they could see that the haystack was blazing furiously. As the train pulled to a stop, the men streamed off the flatcars. All they could do was watch. The fire was out of control.

"Someone's thrown things on the stack!" one of the men shouted. "Boxes and tools!"

"It was set on purpose!"

"Hey, look at the kid," someone said, pointing to Jamie sprawled out on the ground.

"Wasn't he cook's help?"

Meg heard the commotion and came over to see what was going on. She found Jamie rubbing his head and looking around in a confused way. Mr. Henry, Sam and Mason were walking hurriedly towards the growing crowd.

She crouched over him. "How did you get here, Jamie?"

"I saw the smoke, Meg. I ... "

"This boy set the fire!" Mr. Henry was excited. "He's tied up with the Ryans."

"No." Jamie felt confused. "My horse threw me."

"It's part of their effort to ruin the railway!" The cook was appealing to Mr. Mason. "He was mad at me because I fired him. Then he went and got mixed up with them Ryan boys and rode out here today."

"No ... !"

"When we all left he set fire to the haystack."

"I didn't do it!"

"He's guilty, I tell you, Mr. Mason. Things were thrown into that fire on purpose!"

"He's just a boy," said Sam doubtfully.

Jamie was on his feet now. "I came back to help ... I saw the smoke and ... "

"Grab him!" the cook shouted.

Jamie was in a panic. Strong men grasped his arms and held him firmly. "I didn't do it!"

"Hold him. I'm gonna claim that reward!"

Meg appealed to Mr. Mason. "Jamie wouldn't do this, sir."

The superintendent looked at the boy without a hint of expression. Slowly the commotion among the men subsided. "Are you working for the Ryans?" he asked.

Jamie used all of his strength to collect himself. "I'm a stable boy in the hotel, but I didn't set the fire, sir. You have to believe me."

The men murmured in disbelief. Mr. Mason held his hand up for quiet. "Then if you didn't do it, who did?"

"I ... I don't know."

"He's lying!" the cook shouted.

"You've got no proof," said Sam.

"We caught him at the scene of the crime."

"Jamie couldn't throw all of those things onto the fire by himself," argued Meg.

"It's strange, though." The superintendent seemed to be considering what to do.

"You've got to believe me, sir!"

Mr Mason looked at the girl. "We've got no proof, but ... " He studied Jamie for a moment before making his decision. "You'd best get out of here, boy. You've caused enough commotion for one day."

Jamie brushed the dust from his clothes and then went to get his horse. As he left, he heard Mr. Henry say, "You're makin' a big mistake, sir. He's guilty as sin."

"Let me see that bump, Jamie." Meg followed him. She looked at his forehead while the boy gathered up the reins.

"I'm all right."

"What is happening?"

"I ... "

"Tell me the truth."

"But ... "

"Tell me!"

He looked around guiltily. "It's Bobby who's been doing it, Meg," he whispered.

"What?"

"I saw him riding away from the camp just after the haystack was set on fire."

"Are you sure?"

"Absolutely positive. He set that fire. I know it. I'm scared. I'm caught in the middle."

Suddenly Meg was excited. "This is our chance to get the reward money." She gripped her brother's hand tightly. "Don't you see? Now Mother and the others can finally ..."

"But how? I didn't see him set the fire."

"I have an idea." Meg seemed to let her thoughts drift off for a moment. "Come on!" she said decisively.

"Mr Mason! Mr. Mason!" she called as she hurried across the field to the train. Jamie was left with his horse far behind.

The superintendent was talking to Sam at the locomotive. He turned around as the girl hurried up to him.

"Mr. Mason, could Jamie and I see you privately?"

He looked at her suspiciously. "What's it about now?"

"We have to talk to you."

Without waiting for his answer, Meg began leading him towards Jamie. Mason turned. "Sam, you'd better come, too."

As Jamie watched them walking towards him, his heart was beating wildly. What was Meg up to?

"Now, what's this all about?" asked the superintendent as he offered a cigar to the engineer.

"Tell them what happened, Jamie."

"Meg, I'm not sure ... "

"Jamie saw Bobby Ryan riding away from the camp." Meg interrupted excitedly. "He's the one who set the fire."

Mason looked at the boy intently. "Is this true?"

"I'm sorry I didn't tell you before, sir. It's just ... "

The men licked their cigars and lit them.

"Did you actually see him set it, Jamie?" asked the superintendent.

"No. But he was ... well ... riding away as fast as he could."

"Then I don't see what good ... "

"I know we can't prove anything this time," interrupted Meg. "But now we know for sure the Ryans are behind all the trouble. And I've got an idea of how we can trap them."

"What's that?"

"The Ryans want to have a race to prove their stage is faster and better than the railway." She tried to stay calm as she explained. "But they must know they can't win. What they must be planning to do is fix the race."

"We figured that out before," said Sam.

"But now Jamie is working with the Ryan boys. He's with them every day and knows everything they're doing. They trust him. If we set up the race they'll try some trick to make sure they win. Jamie will hear about it and tell us. We'll catch them red-handed."

Jamie looked at Meg, wide-eyed. Things were happening too quickly. What did Meg want him to do? Why hadn't she told him her plans first?

Sam and Mr. Mason glanced at each other. The superintendent puffed thoughtfully on his cigar. "Hmmm ... "

"But Will is sure he can win a race against the train," Jamie blurted.

"Come on, son. Even Will Ryan isn't that stupid," Sam replied.

"But he told me ... "

"What I'm worried about is that equipment might get damaged in this race," the superintendent said.

"It'll never get that far," said Meg. "Jamie will get the information, and we'll trap them before they try anything. That way we'll have all the evidence we need, and the train will still be safe."

"What do you think, Sam?" Mason asked.

"There's already been damage. Somethin' nasty's gonna happen unless we can put a stop to it."

Mason puffed on his cigar. "It's a big risk, that's for sure, but I don't see how we have any choice."

Meg was smiling. "Jamie can arrange to bring the Ryan boys out to the camp tomorrow night to set the terms of the race. Right, Jamie?"

"I ... I guess so," the boy nodded, but he felt deeply uneasy.

"If this works, Mr. Mason," Meg said tentatively, "and we catch them, does it mean we will get the two hundred dollar reward?"

The superintendent smiled. "I said anyone who could stop this damage to the railway would get the money, and I'm a man of my word."

CHAPTER 12

A S Jamie rode back down the concession road to the highway, he tried to think. He was worried. Will Ryan was his friend, and yet he had agreed to Meg's scheme to try to trap him. It seemed terribly dishonest.

Bobby was at the centre of it all. He had set the haystack on fire. He must have been the one who had dropped the tree across the track. But what did Will have to do with it all?

When Jamie got back to town, he half expected to find Bobby waiting for him at the stable, but thankfully the place was deserted. After he had given his horse a rubdown, put him back into his stall and given him a drink of water, he went into the tack room and started sorting through the mess of harnesses and gear. Then he sat on a bench in the sun and began cleaning the leather.

Was Will the one directing Bobby? Why had he helped Jamie get the job in the stable? Was he being used in a plot of the Ryan brothers to ruin the railway?

After lunch the boy took the other two horses out and exercised them. Then he fed them and took them into the courtyard one at a time to give them a brush with a stiff curry comb. The horses seemed to like the sensation of the comb, and didn't mind when he brushed their tangled manes and long tails. By the time he had finished, he was feeling more confident of his ability to handle the big animals. Already he understood something of their likes and dislikes, and now every time he came into the stable, they looked up at him expecting to be fed or given a friendly pat.

Bobby arrived in the mid-afternoon and left his hot and sweaty horse for Jamie to look after. The boy was much relieved when Bobby disappeared into the hotel through the back door, heading for the saloon.

At about five, Mrs. Palmer stuck her head out the kitchen door to shout that Will Ryan and his stage had arrived. Jamie raced around to the front of the hotel and got there just as the team was reined to a stop. He grabbed a horse's halter and gathered the reins.

"Watch they don't step on you," Will called. "Those hooves can turn your feet black and blue."

Nimbly the boy danced out of the way of the horses and then tied them up. He opened the door of the coach for the passengers and unloaded the luggage from the back. When they were finished, he led the horses around to the stable.

"Good trip?" he asked Will.

"Them horses seem to get faster every day."

The boy felt uneasy. He was supposed to set up a meeting between Will and the railroaders to discuss the terms of the race, but he didn't know how to go about it.

"What a change around here," Will said as he looked in through the stable doors. "Did Bobby rub down his own horse?"

"Well, no, I did."

"Lazy … where is that brother of mine?"

"In the saloon, I think."

"Tell him I want to see him. I'm not going to put up with this anymore."

Jamie had never been into the front part of the hotel before, and he found it formidable. There were plush chairs, decorated wallpaper, heavy velvet curtains and Indian rugs. He could hear men in the saloon, and cautiously looked in through the door.

Along one wall was a highly polished mahogany bar with a brass foot-rail. A big spittoon gleamed in the corner. Glasses and liquor bottles stood on the counter behind the bar. On the walls were paintings and photographs of sportsmen and horses, and over the mantlepiece was a massive moose head with a set of antlers easily six feet across. A few tables and chairs were scattered around, but most of the patrons stood at the bar.

Fifteen or more people were in the room, all of them men. Judging from the way they dressed, most were farmers or labourers of some sort. As Jamie came into the darkened room, men turned around to look at him. Gradually the talking slowed and then stopped altogether.

A barman, dressed in a white shirt, narrow bow tie and long white apron, came to the end of the bar. He had a moustache, waxed and curled upwards at the ends, and his black hair was oiled. "No young people allowed in here," he announced.

"I'm the stable boy," Jamie explained. "I'm looking for Bobby Ryan."

The barman pointed across the room. Bobby was sitting alone at a table with a half-empty bottle and small shot glass in front of him. Jamie went over to him.

"Bobby ... ?"

He looked up with bleary eyes. "Whatcha want, kid?"

"Will wants to see you."

"Got somethin' cooked up with him, have you?" He slurred his words drunkenly.

"No."

"Still tied in with the railroad, ain't you, boy. I seen you there."

Jamie felt a sudden panic. "This morning?"

"When else?"

"What were you doing there?"

"That ain't none of your business."

"Bobby, are you drunk again?" Will Ryan towered threateningly over both of them.

"You know this here kid of yours was out at the railroad this mornin', Will? He's a traitor been sent here to spy on us."

"Out at the railroad?" The driver looked confused. "What were you doing there, Jamie?"

The boy was in a panic. "I ... like ... "

"Givin' information to that there Sam Bolt and his railroaders, I bet. The kid's gonna do us in, Will."

"No, I'm not."

"Then why was you out there?"

"My sister Meg is still in the camp. I had to tell her I was working here."

"That girl was the same one who was in town askin' questions about us." Bobby was in triumph. "They're tryin' to hook us on somethin', Will. Real crafty, they are."

"It's not true," Jamie argued. "Why were you out at the camp, Bobby?"

"I was spyin' on you, and it's a good thing, too. You gotta get rid of this kid, Will, before he traps us in somethin'. You know how them railroaders blame us for everything."

Will looked at Jamie. His eyes were hard.

"I did go out there. That's true." The boy knew he had to press ahead to save himself. "And ... and I've got some news for you."

"What's that?"

"The railway wants to have the race."

"What?"

"They want to settle it once and for all to prove the train is faster."

Will was puzzled. "Why would they change their minds now?"

"Sam Bolt always wanted the race. It was Mr. Mason."

"I'd watch this boy if I was you," said Bobby.

"But why now?" asked Will.

"I don't know." Jamie felt terrible to be lying to his friend. "Anyway, they want you to go out to the camp tomorrow night to set the terms. You can ask them yourself."

"It's a trap," said Bobby. "They plan to ambush us or somethin'."

"It's nothing like that."

A smile was coming across the stage driver's face. "Are you telling the truth now, boy?"

"Yes, they want the race, but you've got to be careful. I know those railroaders. They think they can beat you easily with their train."

"Then they know nothin' about Will Ryan and his team of horses. We're gonna run them into the ground."

"Maybe you shouldn't do it," said the boy, half hoping he would back out.

"You don't understand, Jamie. This is our big chance. I've been waitin' and schemin' all summer for it. The race is going to save my stage line."

CHAPTER 13

THAT evening Jamie felt an urge to go to Will and tell him everything. Was it right to betray his friends to help his family? Jamie mulled over the problem as he sat on a bench in the stable, huddled around a lantern, working the saddle soap into the leather of the harnesses. When it was time to climb up into the loft and go to sleep, he still had not decided what to do. All night long he tossed and turned, but when he woke up, it was no better.

As they waited for passengers the next morning, Will said to him, "You go out to the railroad camp this afternoon, Jamie. Try and smell out what's happenin'. See whether this race is on the level. I'll get my brothers together. See you there about seven."

When he climbed up to the box of the stage, he added, "Meet us out on the road leadin' into the camp. I'm countin' on you." Will smiled, full of confidence.

It was a bad day for Jamie. He worried and fretted, turning things over and over in his mind, but he couldn't resolve what to do. In late afternoon he saddled up his cream-coloured horse and rode north to the railway camp. Maybe he should talk things over with Meg to make her understand why he couldn't go along with her plan.

When he saw her in the cook tent, she called to him urgently and hurried outside.

"Jamie ... Jamie, we had a letter from Kate."

"Kate? What does she say?"

Wordlessly, Meg pulled a folded sheet of paper out of her pocket and handed it to her brother. The letter was written in the careful, childlike hand of his eleven-year-old sister.

> Dear Meg and Jamie:
>
> Mother would not like it if she knew I was writing this letter to you.
>
> Things are bad for us. We lost the house. We have no money. And we can not stay at Uncle's any longer because their place is too small.
>
> Mother works washing clothes. Robbie and I sell newspapers every morning but still we don't have enough money.
>
> Can you help us?
>
> Love Kate.

Jamie read the letter over three times before he looked up at his sister. He could see the concern in her eyes.

"We've got to do something, Jamie. Kate wouldn't write unless things were terrible. Maybe they're starving." She put her hand on his arm and glanced around at Mr. Henry. "We've got to win that reward."

"But what if we can't?"

"Of course we can," Meg whispered impatiently. "Now that you've got the job with the Ryans, it'll be easy."

"I don't know."

"What's wrong with you, Jamie?" Meg scowled. "First you wouldn't work around the kitchen. Then you got a soft job in the stable but still you don't seem to care about helping the family."

"I am going to help!"

"I'm working fourteen hours a day. The least you can do is get the information so we can win the reward."

"But, Meg, you don't understand."

"All right, now, you two," barked Mr. Henry. "You've jawed enough. Get back to work, girl, and I want layabouts like you out of my tent." He pointed to Jamie.

The boy went outside to wait. He wanted to be as far away from the tyrannical cook as possible. In fact, he wanted to be as far away from the railroad camp as possible.

Meg annoyed him. She seemed almost resentful of the fact that he had a job that he liked, and she didn't see that Will Ryan could be a decent, honest man. It was unfair of her to accuse him of not caring about the family. He wanted to see Mother and the others again as much as she did. But did that mean he had to betray his friends?

It was after the men had gone in for supper that Jamie got ready to head out to meet the Ryan boys. He climbed into the saddle and was about to ride away when he saw Sam and Mr. Mason coming to the cook tent.

"Where are you goin', boy?" the engineer called to him.

"I arranged to meet the Ryans on the road."

The two men talked for a moment, casting suspicious looks at Jamie.

"Your sister will go with you," Mr. Mason announced finally.

"I'll be all right."

"This country ain't safe," said Sam hastily. "Meg ... Meg ... " He went into the tent to find her.

A couple of minutes later Meg had shed her apron and climbed up on the horse behind him. As they were riding down the wagon road, Mason called after them.

"Be careful of those Ryan boys. Remember, they can be dangerous."

The warmth of the afternoon lingered in the air, but the evening quiet was already beginning to settle. The country was as flat as a lake. The men were laying over half a mile of track a day now, but Mr. Mason said they would have to do better than that if they were going to finish the steel to Wingham before winter set in.

"Maybe we shouldn't have got involved in all of this," said Jamie suddenly.

"If we can get the reward money, it will all be worthwhile."

"But, Meg ... "

"The Ryans won't bother us. Don't worry so much."

Jamie was silent. It seemed that he couldn't even talk to Meg anymore. She was so concerned about the reward money, she probably didn't even care that he had to lie to Will to set up the race.

On the concession road, near the tracks, a big elm tree grew by the fence line, its crown spreading out like a broad umbrella. Under the tree was a soft grassy spot. They sat down and propped themselves up against the split rail fence that snaked beside the road. Neither of them spoke.

Jamie lay with his arms behind his head and watched a large hawk circling lazily in the sky. Suddenly it seemed to hesitate in mid-air and dropped like a stone, going faster and faster as it sped towards the earth. A few feet from the ground the big bird spread its wings and swooped. Then, with powerful flaps, it began to rise, carrying the struggling form of a mouse in its talons.

The sun was sinking lower. Shadows lengthened, and a hush settled on the countryside. Suddenly Jamie sat upright. "Hear that? Hooves!" He stood up and looked down the road. "Here they come!"

The four Ryan brothers were riding their horses in an easy canter towards them. Will was out in front on a big black animal with a white star on its forehead. he rode with one hand holding the reins and the other on his hip, his eyes restlessly moving about, looking for any sign of trouble.

Riding beside him on his bay gelding was Bobby. He wore a sloppy, misshapen felt hat that drooped around the rim. Behind them rode the other two brothers, sitting high in their saddles. With every pound of the hooves the men and horses grew larger until Will and Bobby reined up, towering over the pair standing by the road.

"What have we got here?" said Bobby as he circled his horse in behind them.

"Is this your sister?" asked Will.

"Yeah, it's Meg."

"Guess you know Bobby. These here other two are Frank and Tom."

All four of the men were carrying weapons. Will and Tom wore revolvers strapped to their hips and rifles held in long holsters on the saddles. Frank had a rifle and Bobby carried a powerful-looking shotgun.

"Expecting trouble?" Meg asked calmly, nodding at the weapons.

"We found out before that it's best to be ready with them railroaders," Will smiled. "Is the race set up?"

"You have to talk to Sam Bolt," Meg replied. "He's waiting at the camp."

Will laughed. "That engine man's gonna eat the dust of my stage."

Bobby and Frank were dancing their horses around in a high-spirited way, coming dangerously close to the two young people. Jamie shied back to avoid the big animals. Bobby's laughter mocked him. Suddenly he gave his horse a kick. The animal reared back momentarily, then wheeled and began to circle Jamie and Meg. In an instant Tom followed him, and then Frank joined the tight circle of horses rushing around the two figures in the middle of the road.

Meg and Jamie held onto each other as they tried to avoid the animals and their pounding hooves. The more frightened they looked, the more the brothers laughed, and the harder they rode their horses. Tighter and tighter the circle drew. The thunder of the hooves, the giant animals and the mocking laughter filled Meg and Jamie with fear.

The crack of a gun broke the spell. In Will's hand was a smoking revolver. "Enough!" We've got business in the railroad camp. Get your horse, boy, and let's go."

In the next moment Will brought his horse to Meg's side. He leaned down, scooped her up with one arm, and swung her onto the horse's back behind him. Jamie ran to climb aboard his mount. Then, with shouts, the five horses galloped down the wagon road.

As the horses thundered into the camp, the railroad labourers dropped what they were doing and began to gather. Will reined to a stop in front of the cook tent.

"Sam Bolt!" he shouted. "Is Sam Bolt the engineer there, or did he turn tail and run when he saw us comin'?"

The canvas flap to the cook tent pulled back and Sam appeared flanked by his conductor and the other trainmen. Mr. Mason stood off to one side, listening.

"I'm here, and I'm gonna stay here, just like the railroad." The engineer walked across the dusty yard towards the horsemen.

"We'll see about that," Will replied. "After I get finished racing that fire-eatin' bucket o' bolts, you might wish you'd never come to this part of the country."

Sam had folded his arms across his stomach. "My train can beat your stage any day of the week."

"Then it's a race we've got," Will smiled. "We're gonna settle this thing once and for all."

A hundred or more men circled the horses now. They stood silent and hostile. Bobby pulled out his shotgun and held it across his lap. The other brothers watched the crowd of railroaders tensely.

The stage driver was reaching into his jacket pocket. "I got fifty dollars here that says I'm gonna beat that steam-driven pile of junk. You match it, and we've got ourselves a race." He held the bills in his hand and waved them for all to see.

"The winner takes all," Sam snarled.

"We race the day after tomorrow," Will announced in a loud voice. "The start is London at two in the afternoon. That's my normal run, and I'll be carrying a full load of passengers up to Exeter. To make it fair, the train will have to be haulin' a full load as well. The first to arrive in this here camp will win."

"You'd better be prepared to lose," said Sam.

Will laughed. "If you think we're gonna lose, you know nothin' about the Ryan brothers."

He jerked the reins and his big animal wheeled around. Hooves pounded on the hard-packed earth. Bobby reined his animal to follow him, and then the others spurred their mounts as they thundered out of the camp. Jamie kicked his horse to keep up. In a moment the five horses were racing at a full gallop back down the wagon road. The brothers were laughing and yelling like wild men.

CHAPTER 14

THE next morning, Will arranged to have Bobby drive the stage to London while he got things ready for the race. After they had seen him off, he went back to the stable with Jamie and set to work. There was a jumbled pile of harnesses in the tack room that the boy had ignored. The two hauled them out to the courtyard and started to untangle them.

"This is part of the secret of how we're gonna win this race, Jamie boy," Will said with excitement in his voice.

"How's that?"

"Don't you be tellin' anybody now, but this here harness is for a four-horse team."

"You mean ... ?"

"That's it. With an extra two horses on the stage, we'll be able to race up them hills in a full gallop." He laughed. "That Sam Bolt thinks he's so smart, but there ain't no flies on us Ryan boys."

Jamie couldn't help smiling. "Do you think you might be able to win fair and square, Will?"

"What do you mean think? I know it."

"Wow!"

"And it's not just gonna be me. We're gonna do it together. You're part of our outfit now — one of the Ryan boys." He gave Jamie a good-natured punch on the arm. "But enough of this talkin'. We've got a powerful lot of work to get things in shape for tomorrow's run. Let's get crackin'."

Jamie felt terrible. Will saw him as part of a team effort to defeat the railroad, and yet he was supposed to be working with Meg to see the stage defeated. He was more dishonest than anyone in this whole affair.

He wanted to tell Will about the plan of the railroad, but he knew if he did that it would finish the race and any chance of winning the reward money. Worse still, it would prove that Bobby had been right about him all along. He was no more than a spy for the railroad.

"Come on, boy," Will said when he noticed Jamie staring absently at the harnesses. "Let's get the old elbow grease workin'."

First they spread the harness out on the ground, untangling it as they went, and then Will began a careful inspection of every inch of the leather. Jamie started cleaning and polishing the harness with saddle soap while Will got out needle and thread and began to stitch up the small tears and pulls that seemed to be everywhere.

"Bobby let this harness rot into ruin," said the stage driver. "Work lots of that soap into her, boy. That'll soften her up and get her back into shape."

"Your brother doesn't ... seem to like to ... work," said Jamie uncertainly.

"He was the baby of the family. Grew up in the shadow of three high-spirited brothers. A thing like that's enough to give anyone problems. He's still findin' his own way."

As they worked, Will began to talk about the race. He was very keyed up.

"It's a funny thing. That railroad is a great huge company, and they must have plenty of real smart people workin' for 'em, but they've made one mistake, boy, one big mistake, and they can't even see it."

"What's that?"

"They're over-confident. They think they can win this race without half tryin', but it ain't gonna work that way. That track still is in mighty poor shape. There are parts of it that aren't ballasted, and the trains have to go slowly over the bridges. Sam Bolt just can't steam up the line full throttle all the way."

"The other thing they haven't figured out yet is that I'm gonna be drivin' the best teams of horses in the whole of southwestern Ontario." Will laughed. "I've been talkin' to the owners and drivers of other stage lines in the area. They're all worried about this railway business, and they're gonna help us win by lendin' their best horses. Tomorrow we're gonna have the fastest teams that have ever been assembled in these parts. I tell you, boy. Them railway men are in for the surprise of their lives."

Jamie listened carefully as he continued working the saddle soap into the stiff leather. It sounded as if Will Ryan had a well-thought-out strategy based on good horses, hard driving and knowledge of the competition. He was going to win the race fair and square!

But where did that leave Meg, and her plans to win the reward? She had told him she would be coming into town to find out how the Ryan boys were going to wreck the train. What was he going to tell her? And what would happen to their family if they didn't win the reward? How could they get the money they needed unless Meg's scheme worked?

"I tell you, Jamie boy, it's gonna be sweet to win this race." Will smiled broadly. "That railroad gang think of themselves as the big city boys, and the Ryans are the country bumpkins. They think we know nothin'. Tomorrow they're gonna get a big surprise when us poor, stupid country folk whomp them good and proper." He laughed.

They worked on the harnesses together for a couple of hours. By then Will had finished all of the repairs, and the rest was left to Jamie. Will went into the stable, brought out Bobby's riding horse, and saddled him up.

"I've got to ride south to organize the teams of horses for the race, Jamie. Tonight, after Bobby gets back, we've gotta work on the coach until she runs just perfect." He was about to mount his horse when he paused.

"By the way, I meant to tell you what a good job you're doin'. You put out far more work than my own brother, Bobby, and you've got some brains behind it, too. Tomorrow I want you ridin' on the stage with me during the race. You can handle the passengers and mail. Then I can spend my time thinkin' about the horses. How does that sound?"

"Sure. Great. Anything to help."

Will swung into the saddle. "Good. I'll arrange it with Mr. Gage when I get back. See you then." With a wave he was gone.

Jamie continued to work, sitting in the sun in the courtyard. Meg was counting on him to give her information to trap the Ryans so that they could get the reward and save the family. But as far as he knew, Will was going to run an honest race.

Finally Jamie finished working on the harnesses and then took the gear into the stable. Rather than dumping it back in a heap, he hung it neatly on pegs so it could be easily taken down without becoming tangled. Afterwards he went back to his other chores, exercising the horses, cleaning their stalls and feeding them.

It was late afternoon when the stage rushed up the street to complete its run. Jamie hurried out to grab the horses and guide them to the hitching post. The big animals were covered in sweat, and their mouths were foaming. They had been run hard.

As Bobby climbed to the ground he was unsteady on his feet. "Look after them horses, kid. I need a little liquid refreshment to chase the road dust from my throat." He navigated up the porch and in through the big hotel doors. The boy could hear him ordering a whisky all the way out onto the street.

Jamie steered the horses back into the courtyard and unhitched the coach in a place where he and Will could work on it easily. Then he took the harnesses off the horses and rubbed them down.

Suddenly there was a shout. "Get my horse saddled there, boy!" It was Bobby staggering drunkenly on the back porch of the hotel.

"I can't do that."

"And why not? You're a stable boy, ain't you?"

"Will took your horse south this morning. He's not back yet."

"Took my horse? He ain't got no right to do that." Bobby was lurching across the courtyard. He looked in through the door of the stable, trying to see what other animals were still in their stalls.

At that moment Jamie was leading one of the coach horses into the stable. "Mind yourself, Bobby."

"You mind your own self, good for nothin' kid," he muttered to himself.

Jamie tied the horse up in the stall and then went back to get the other. Bobby was talking more to himself than anyone else.

"You're a no-good traitor, ain't you, boy?"

"What's that?"

"Still a railway man, I bet."

The boy got the other horse and started leading him into the stable. He knew Bobby was drunk. "Watch yourself again."

Bobby stumbled as he backed up against the stable door to get out of the way. "Are you tryin' to push me around?"

"I told you to be careful."

"Don't tell me what to do, kid!" He waved his fist. "After I'm finished, you'd be nothin' but a grease spot on the ground."

Jamie watered and fed the horses, trying to ignore the rantings. Why did Bobby want to make trouble for him all the time?

"Saddle me up one of them other horses," Bobby suddenly ordered. He was leaning up against the stable door, weaving back and forth. His eyes were so bleary that he was finding it difficult to focus.

Jamie found it hard to believe that anyone could drink so much in such a short time. Bobby had been driving the stage for most of the day, and he hadn't been in the saloon for more than fifteen minutes. Then the boy noticed a brown whisky bottle sticking out of Bobby's back pocket.

"I said I want a horse, boy!" Bobby bellowed. "Now snap to it!"

"You're too drunk."

"Who are you to tell me what to do? I wanna horse! I want that white one right there. Now saddle him up for me!!"

The cream-coloured horse was Jamie's. He was not going to let this drunken man ride it. "No!" he said decisively. "You're not fit to ride anything."

Bobby swayed dangerously and took a couple of steps towards the boy. "I've had enough from you." He was slurring his words, but it didn't stop his tirade. "You come in here and mess up my stable and turn my brother Will against me. Then you tell me I ain't gonna ride one of them horses. I've been in the saddle since I was a boy of five and nobody tells me when I'm fit to ride!"

"What do you need a horse for? Are you planning to go out and cause more trouble at the railway?"

"What's it to you?"

"Gonna drop a tree across the track?" Jamie taunted. "Or maybe there's another haystack you want to set fire to."

Bobby lurched forward. "You can't talk to me like that, kid."

"Maybe you're going to kill somebody next time, Bobby. Is that how you plan to win the race?"

"Somebody's gotta win the thing." He had taken his bottle out of his pocket and took a swig from it. Then he wiped his mouth with his sleeve. "The railway's too fast. She's gonna bury our stage. Then what are we gonna do?"

"So you're going to find a way to stop the train tomorrow."

"Will won't do it! He's got some fool idea that we can beat the thing in a race — special four-horse teams and all that stuff. It won't do any good against that steam machine. If it weren't for me we wouldn't have a prayer."

"How are you going to do it?"

Bobby took another quick drink. "Can't be a coward in this world, boy. Gotta be tough and hard. Will taught me that. Will and my other brothers. For years I was the smallest of the Ryan boys. People laughed at me, and I always had to try harder than any of the others. But this time I'm the one settin' the pace. I'm gonna win this race for Will and the whole family so we can save the stage line." He smiled with a crazy, drunken look. "I'm gonna be the hero of the day." He threw his head back and drained what was left of the bottle.

"I bet you are," Jamie muttered.

"Everybody's gonna know Bobby Ryan after this. They're gonna say Bobby's the real leader of the Ryan boys. He's the one with brains and guts. He deserves the respect." He laughed crazily. "I'm gonna get a drink."

He weaved across the courtyard, a pathetic drunk who had suddenly forgotten what he had wanted to do. "A drink. Gimme a drink." He lurched up onto the back porch of the hotel and disappeared through the door.

Jamie leaned against the stable door gathering his thoughts. Bobby was the one who had been behind the railroad's problems. Will knew nothing about it. More important, Jamie had learned that Bobby planned to do something during the race.

The boy smiled to himself. Yes, now he knew what to do next.

CHAPTER 15

THE stable was quiet. The only sound was of the horses foraging in the hay. Occasionally there was a sharp, hard thump as one of the big animals clumped its foot on the floor.

Slowly the stable door opened and Bobby slipped inside. In the dim light he was no more than an uncertain shadow, silently moving from the spot where they stored the tools to the front door and back again. He collected an axe, a saw and a pick, left them by the door and went to get his horse.

They could hear him whispering softly to the animal. Then he backed him out of the stall and led him to the stable entrance. Opening the door a crack so he could see better, Bobby slipped the bit into the horse's mouth and went to get the blanket and saddle.

"Goin' somewhere?"

Bobby jumped in fright. "Will! You scared me. Whatcha doin' here?"

"What are you doin'?"

The younger brother looked around guiltily. "Just goin' for a ride. Thought I'd go out and get some fresh air. You know ... "

"What have you got them tools for, then?" Will's mouth was set in a hard frown.

"Well, I donno ... like. I was just gonna ... "

"Yeah?"

"Take 'em to a friend." Bobby was wary.

"Was that friend out on the railway line?"

"The railway? Why'd you say that?"

"'Cause Jamie here says you've got plans to wreck the train tomorrow."

The boy came out of the shadows and stood beside the two Ryan brothers. Bobby looked at him and then back at his brother. His face was red and flushed, and his eyes had a bloodshot, watery look about them. "I wasn't goin' nowhere, Will. Really I wasn't."

"I figure you have some scheme to help with the race," said Jamie.

"Were you plannin' to wreck the rail line?" Will demanded harshly.

"No ... no, I wasn't, Will ... honest!"

Jamie remained calm. "You told me you thought Will was going to need all the help he could get."

"Why don't you shut up, kid!" Bobby's voice cracked with emotion.

"Were you gonna damage the track?" Will demanded.

"No ... really!!" He cowered back against the wall.

"You told me that Will couldn't win the race on his own. You needed to give him some help," Jamie insisted.

"Is that right, Bobby?"

The younger brother was looking from one to the other. Finally he burst out, "The life of the stage line is runnin' on this race, Will! If we lose we've lost everythin'. You know that we can't win just with horses and the stage! They'll bury us!"

"So you were going to help out a little!" Jamie pressed. "Is that it?"

"I'll get you, kid!!" Bobby lunged for the boy, but Will slammed him against the side of one of the stalls.

"Stop that!" the stage driver shouted.

"Were you going to drop another tree across the track?" Jamie demanded.

Will grabbed his brother by the shirt front and shook him hard. "Tell us what you were gonna do!! Tell me before I lose my temper!"

"You never listen to me, Will!" Bobby began to tremble. "You can't beat that train. It's too fast."

Will shook him again. "So you were just gonna equal up the odds a little."

"You were always tellin' me what to do! You won't ever let me do nothin' on my own! I was just tryin' to help!" Tears wet his cheeks.

"What were you gonna do?"

"The bridge."

"The bridge over the Sable River?"

"Yeah," he whimpered.

"What were you going to do?" Will waited. The veins on his neck stood out. His hands twisted Bobby's shirt. "What were you going to do?!"

"The pillars," Bobby whispered.

"What?!!"

"I was gonna cut the pillars."

"Cut the pillars. My God, Bobby, how could you?"

Jamie was horrified. "It's a hundred foot drop off that bridge. People would have been killed. Sam ... Meg ... "

Will was shaking his head as if he couldn't believe what he had heard. "I always figured you were just a young buck rushin' around the country sowin' your wild oats, but this ... this is terrible."

"I just wanted to help, Will."

"Your idea of help is close to murder. If you carry on, Bobby, people here abouts will get so mad at the Ryan boys there's no tellin' where it will lead."

"Are you gonna turn me over to the police?"

"Maybe I should turn you over to the railroad."

"Don't do that. Please!"

"You deserve it, but I can't do that. But I'll tell you this. Until the race is over you're gonna stick to me like glue on wallpaper." He threw back the stable doors and stepped out into the courtyard. "Tomorrow you're going to come down to London with us, Bobby. During the race you can be an outrider goin' ahead to each of the post horse stations to see everythin's ready."

"Anythin' you say, Will. I'll do anythin'." He looked truly sorry for what he had done.

"Right now, we're gonna fix up the coach until she runs smooth as a clock. Come on, you two. Let's get a move on. We've got a lot to do before she gets dark."

The coach was a light vehicle built for speed. Will and Bobby got at the front right wheel and lifted it up until Jamie could get a saw horse under the axle. Quickly Will undid the bolts holding the wheel in place and pulled it off. Bobby greased up the shaft, and then they put the wheel back and tightened the bolts.

As they worked, Jamie became increasingly worried. He had been so involved trying to find out Bobby's plans that he had half forgotten that Meg was going to come into town after supper to find out what the Ryans were going to do.

The problem was that Jamie didn't know what he was going to tell his sister. He was one of the Ryans now. The railway was the opposition, and he wanted to defeat them as badly as Will or Bobby or any of the others. And yet there was still that reward. What was he going to do?

The work on the stage didn't take long to finish. They moved from wheel to wheel, lifting up the coach, pulling off each wheel, greasing up the shaft and bolting the wheel back in place again. Once they were done, Will began a thorough inspection of every moving part on the coach. It took an hour or more, but finally he declared that the stage was in top shape.

"If we ain't ready for this race now we'll never be," he said to Jamie and Bobby. "Let's get ourselves some sleep. Tomorrow's a big day."

Will and Bobby went into the hotel where they had rooms, while Jamie cleared up the tools and tidied the stable. It was getting dark now, and the boy had to light a lantern. What was he going to tell Meg? If he said that the Ryans were going to run the race fair and square, not only would there be no reward, but maybe Mr. Mason would insist that the contest be called off. Will really wanted the race. If it was cancelled it would dash all of his hopes of showing that his stage was faster than the train.

"Pssst ... Jamie. Douse the lantern." Meg had slipped in through the door and was standing in the yellow light, smiling at her brother. "We don't want them to see us."

"You're late," he whispered as he blew out the flame. An uneasy darkness settled over them.

"I got here awhile ago and saw you working with Will and Bobby," she whispered. "I thought they'd never go away."

"I was trying to hurry them. Will wanted to get the coach in top running order."

"He's not stupid enough to think he has a chance in this race, is he?"

"There's nothing stupid about Will," Jamie bristled.

"Stupid and arrogant. The railway men are still talking about how the Ryans came out to the camp with their guns."

"They felt threatened."

"Those brothers are just a bunch of outlaws who go around the countryside causing trouble."

"They are not, Meg. How can you say that? You don't know anything about them."

"Soon it's going to be over, Jamie. I wrote Mother to tell her that help is on the way. We're going to get the reward and then everything will be fine."

"I don't know about this, Meg."

"What do you mean you don't know? You did get the information, didn't you?"

Jamie could feel his stomach tense. "Do you mean about the race?"

"Of course about the race! Are you getting stupid?" she said sharply. "Didn't you find out?"

"It's the bridge," he blurted.

"The bridge? What do you mean?"

Jamie could hear his heart beating. Sweat was gathering on his forehead. "The Sable River bridge a couple of miles north of town. You know the one. Bobby plans to cut the pillars."

Meg took a sharp intake of air. "The train would plunge a hundred feet or more down to the river. Everyone could be killed."

"What are you going to do, Meg?"

"We're going to catch them red-handed. You just wait until they try to attack the bridge. They'll be so surprised, they won't know what happened to them."

CHAPTER 16

SAM Bolt was organizing the train to London even before breakfast was finished. When the steam was up in the locomotive, he gave a long blast on the whistle, and Meg and others hurried to climb aboard.

Mr. Mason was giving the engineer last-minute instructions. "Now don't get too involved in this thing, Sam. Remember, we're going to catch them here at the bridge. Just ride up the line nice and easy, like it was a normal day's run. We'll do the rest."

"And Meg," the superintendent continued. "You just sit there and keep out of everyone's way. If anything comes up with that brother of yours, you'll have to deal with it. I don't exactly trust him."

Sam was smiling. "Sure will be good to see them Ryan boys behind bars. This thing has been goin' on far too long."

The engineer checked his gauges. The fireman, a man by the name of Brit, threw a few more logs into the flames, the bell began to ring, and the engine shuddered and chugged. Slowly it began to move. Soon they crossed the Sable River bridge, passed through the outskirts of Exeter and headed south through the rich farmland.

Meg leaned out of the window on the lefthand side of the cab, watching the country roll by. She was keyed up and yet calm all at the same time. Everything was in place. The Ryan boys would be caught, she and Jamie would win the reward, and the family would finally be reunited.

The train passed a large farmhouse built of white brick. Freshly painted delicate ornamental gingerbread decorated the eaves and the porch. As the train steamed past, Meg could see children out in the yard. She waved, and a young boy and girl smiled and waved back.

To have the family together, happy and secure, just like those people in the farmhouse. That was what Meg wanted more than anything else in the world. Maybe now it would be possible.

When they arrived in London it was still only nine-thirty in the morning. Sam was anxious to get organized. "I'm goin' in to see the yard foreman about our old engine," he told the others.

"Can I come?" Meg asked.

"Sure, girl. Hustle it up now."

They picked their way through the yard, stepping over tracks and dodging around freight cars, until they came to a roundhouse and an enormous series of sheds just off Egerton Street.

Sam left Meg watching a crew of men working on a passenger car that had been smashed in an accident of some kind. One whole side had caved in, windows were broken, and the wood paneling was crushed. The men were tearing the car apart and completely rebuilding it.

As she waited, Meg wandered over to another section of the yard where they were working on locomotives. Boilermakers were sealing up the joints in an engine that had just been brought in. Another had its boiler completely removed, and a group of men were getting ready to hoist a new one onto the old frame.

This was a big yard where three hundred men worked in twelve-hour shifts, repairing damage and keeping the running stock of the railway in good order. There were at least a half dozen engines in the shop, and maybe twenty railway cars being repaired.

It was ten minutes or more before Sam came out of the office. "They say old 151 is as fit as she ever was. I just wish we were racin' the Ryans for real. It's the fastest locomotive of its size in the company."

They found the engine parked on one of the sidings. Sam got a yard locomotive to haul 151 down to the water tower and fill up her boiler. Then, with it parked on a siding, Brit fired her up. While waiting, they began cleaning and polishing every available part of the engine.

First they worked on the big brass straps that went all the way around the boiler at the seams. Then the boiler itself was blackened to protect it from rust. Meg was given the job of cleaning the big brass bell, and she rubbed away at it until it gleamed.

When the boiler was hot, Sam examined the seams to see if there were any leaks. Whenever he found any tell-tale sign of moisture, he hammered a resin sealer into the place where the metal came together until he was satisfied that the seam was water-tight.

Brit put oil and tallow on the pistons and connecting rods and every other moving part on the locomotive. Then they stacked dry ash, birch and maple into the tender. Before long, Sam was shunting his engine back and forth on the sidings as he collected the freight cars that they would be taking up to the construction camp.

Meg happened to look out towards York Street and saw the stagecoach drawing to a stop at the curb. "Look! The Ryans have got a four-horse team. Jamie didn't tell me about that."

Sam cursed under his breath. "If that ain't the limit. Those lying Ryans will do anything to make us think they're on the level. Well, if he wants to put on this little show … come on."

The engineer jumped down from the cab and strode across the tracks towards the street. Meg scrambled to keep up with him. Sam was shouting even before he got to the coach.

"I've had it with your swindles, Ryan. You don't know how to play fair!"

Will sat up on top of his stage holding the reins in one hand and balancing his long horse whip in the other. He looked proud and hostile. Beside him was Jamie looking distinctly uncomfortable.

"What are you talkin' about, Bolt?"

"Them horses. You never said nothin' about havin' a four-horse team."

"I didn't hear no rules against it. It's just a race between your train and my stagecoach."

"Well, you couldn't beat me even if you had an eight-horse team. We're not only tougher than you, Ryan, but the railway is a whole lot smarter. You'll see."

"Time will tell the tale," Will laughed. "I just came down to show off my rig and to check if you was ready for the race."

"We're ready."

"Good, 'cause I aim to collect the wager as soon as I get to the railway camp." Will's high-spirited horses were starting to get restless. They rocked the stage forward and back. "First one into the camp. That's the only rule of this race. Winner takes all. It's two o'clock at the Richmond Street train crossing that we start."

"Don't be late. I can't tie up the traffic on the main line even for a lousy race with you."

The whip cracked over the heads of the horses, and they lurched forward. "I'll be there." The stagecoach wheeled down the street, spewing up dust from its big back wheels. By the time it got to the first corner, the horses were in full gallop.

When Will reined up in front of the City Hotel, he climbed to the ground and began pacing back and forth on the boardwalk. Several times he pulled his big gold pocket watch from his pocket and studied it.

Finally it was time. "Let's get movin', Jamie. She's fifteen minutes before the hour."

The boy began collecting the money from the passengers and packing their luggage while Will went to find his brother. Jamie could hear the exchange.

"If you leave now, and ride like the devil, you'll be ten minutes ahead of us, Bobby. Tell the stable boys to have them horses harnessed up and ready to make the change in two minutes flat. Understand?"

"Sure, Will."

"Then move!" Bobby was about to climb onto his horse when his brother grabbed him by the arm. "If you drink today or mess around with that railroad, I'll tack your hide to the barn door. Do you hear me?"

"I heard." Bobby swung his leg over his horse, smacked its rear with the reins and took off at a hard gallop.

Again Will paced the boardwalk, looking at his big pocket watch every minute. At three minutes before the hour, he shouted, "All aboard!" and climbed up to the driver's box.

Jamie untied the team from the hitching post and held them by the halter. Will looked at his watch one last time. The horses shied nervously. Suddenly he called, "High up!!" The whip cracked. Jamie danced out of the way. The big animals lurched forward. The boy ran, grabbed a hand hold and jumped to get his foot on the bottom rung of the ladder. He was still climbing as they skidded around the corner onto York Street.

It had taken minutes for Sam to get his train through the series of switches. But at two minutes to two, the train was on the main line gathering speed.

They were coming up to the Richmond Street crossing. Sam peered out his window, looking for the stage. Meg climbed back into the tender. There were a number of wagons and horses, but where was Will Ryan?

There he was! She could see the stage racing along York Street. Beside Will, high up on the box, was Jamie.

At the corner, Will pulled hard on his reins, and the stage skidded around the corner onto Richmond and began to head north. Then, with one long, fluid movement, the whip cracked over the horses' heads, and the animals leapt into a gallop.

At the same moment that the stage turned the corner, Sam opened the throttle of locomotive 151. Smoke belched from the big onion-shaped stack. The machine chugged and shuddered as it gathered speed. A long blast of the whistle split the air.

CHAPTER 17

THE four horses raced up Richmond Street, their hooves pounding the hard-packed road, the big spoked wheels kicking up a plume of dust. Will Ryan held four reins in each hand and still managed to crack the air over the horses' heads with his long whip. He drove relentlessly, never letting the animals slacken speed for a moment

Jamie clutched the seat of the stage. The uneven roadway and the speed of the coach gave a fearful rolling that promised at any moment to pitch him off his high perch.

The horses galloped through the city, overtaking slower carts and wagons, and sending pedestrians hurrying for the boardwalks. At busy intersections Will shouted a warning but refused to slow down.

North of the city the coach crossed the river and began the mile-long climb up the hill on the other side. This was the real test of the horses. Will tried to keep them at a gallop. He watched each animal carefully and whenever one of them slackened speed he used his whip to sting the air just over their head. But they couldn't keep to the pace. By the time they were three-quarters of the way up the grade, they had slowed to a trot and all the curses of the driver would not make them go faster.

Will glowered at the animals. "We've got to go faster or that steam machine will be up the line before we get to Arva. Look, even a storm's brewin'.''

Billowing black clouds were blowing in from the west, darkening the sky. Jamie knew that a downpour would turn the roads into a muddy mess and slow the stage.

When they got to the top of the hill, the whip sang and the horses began to gallop again, but they were so played out that they had little speed. At the first changing station, all the animals were bathed in sweat, their mouths foaming. It was only when Will swung them around to the back of the hotel that he brightened. A fresh team of four horses was harnessed and waiting.

"Don't bother gettin' out," he called to the passengers. "We ain't here for long." He was true to his word. In less than two minutes they were back out on the road, galloping northwards.

As the train left London, the crew was completely confident. "Did you see that Will Ryan?" laughed Sam. "He was holdin' onto them reins like grim death."

Meg kept a sharp eye out on the track ahead as they steamed along. She knew it wasn't really a race, but she would have been happier if they were going just a little faster. Sam seemed to be content to doodle along. North of Hyde Park much of the track was unballasted, and the train was carrying a heavy load of rails and ties.

Looking out the window of the cab, the girl noticed for the first time that the sky had darkened. Already there were storm clouds blowing in from the west. The trees were beginning to bend with the wind, and there was a cool nip to the air.

They went through the town of Ilderton and had to get up speed to climb the hill coming out of Brecon. When they crested the rise, Meg leaned out of the window to get a better look at the track. They were in Ryan country, now. It would be best not to take chances.

The girl looked up at the wild, dark sky. Clouds seethed and churned. When they passed a concession road the wind was whipping the dust into little eddies.

The Ryan stage had thundered northward at a faster gallop once they had changed horses. Jamie handled the mail by throwing it off the coach at the storefront post offices along the way, but Will didn't even slow down. The coach went north on the Proof Line Road, pausing briefly at Elginfield to let off a passenger in front of Farrell's Inn. Then they were off again.

At Lucan another team of horses was harnessed and waiting. Will pulled up in front of the hotel, and there was a mad rush to make the change.

"Fastest time you've ever made on this run, Will," the stable boy said.

"We've gotta go even faster."

"Your brothers left on horseback about five minutes ago. Said they'd see you in Exeter."

The driver was climbing up to the box. "All aboard!" he shouted. New passengers hurried to scramble inside the coach. The whip cracked and the fresh team of horses shot ahead, jerking the stage and bouncing the customers about.

A couple of miles out of town they came to the Ausable River. Will was careful taking the road down to the bottom of the gully, but then whipped his horses into a gallop. The four strong animals strained into their collars, snorting and whinnying with the effort, as they took the steep grade.

"We've got ourselves a real team this time, boy," Will shouted. "She'll be a wild ride."

Once they were up the hill the countryside was as flat as a billiard table. The driver cracked his whip once … twice … three times. They were flying along now, kicking up an enormous cloud of dust on the dry road. But the wind was blowing up into gusts, tossing the trees and whipping weeds over the barren fields. Cattle and horses were heading towards the barns to find shelter.

They were taking the turn at Clandeboye when they spotted the train. It was a little behind them, just going through the village. The big onion-shaped stack billowed black smoke into the air, and the sound of the wheels on the steel rails could be heard all the way to the coach.

As Sam saw the stage, he blew a long blast of the steam whistle. The horses pricked up their ears in fright. Will clutched the reins, trying to control them. For a moment it looked as if the team would run off the road, but then they seemed to shake their fears and raced even harder.

"We're beatin' 'em, boy!!" Will shouted excitedly. "See that? We're ahead!!"

It was as if Sam Bolt, in the cab of his locomotive, had heard what Will had said. "If he wants a race, we're gonna give it to him." He was laughing. "Throw on more logs, Brit. I want all the steam I can get out of this machine."

The train coasted for a minute, and then it rushed faster and faster along the track, gathering speed with every thrust of the powerful pistons. The big machine rolled ahead of the stage with ease. Sam blew a long blast on the whistle. The coach horses looked around wildly and galloped all the harder, but it did no good. The engineer played with the stagecoach. He slowed his locomotive down until the horses came up abreast of them, and then he blew his whistle and steamed past again.

We can't go faster than him, Jamie," Will shouted in despair.

"Let's not give up."

Will's only reply was to crack the whip. The animals were a strong, well-co-ordinated team, and they ate up the miles, but by the time they entered the outskirts of Exeter, the train was half a mile ahead.

Bobby, Tom and Frank were waiting outside the hotel with a team of horses harnessed and ready to go. Will pulled to a stop, the passengers scrambled out, thankful to escape the wild ride, and moments later the coach and fresh team were racing north on the highway again.

As the train went through the outskirts of Exeter, Sam began to brake. By the time they saw the Sable River bridge, they were down to a walking pace.

Meg climbed out on the running board so she could see better. This was where the Ryan boys were to be trapped by the hidden railway men. All that remained was to announce the capture, and the reward would be theirs.

Above them, the weather worsened. The wind was whipping at the trees. Birds scuttled for shelter. Heavy drops slanted out of big dark clouds. Somewhere out over Lake Huron, to the west of them, thunder rumbled and rolled.

As they drew to a stop, Mr. Mason, flanked by two of his foremen, came out of the ravine. They hurried to the engine.

"Did you catch them?" Sam called expectantly.

At that moment there was a shout from upriver. The highway bridge across the river was no more than a hundred yards to the east. Will Ryan's stage and his four-horse team thundered over the wooden floor of the bridge. The sound echoed down the gully of the river to the railroaders standing by the bridge.

"We're ahead of 'em, Will!!" they could hear Jamie shout. "We're gonna win!" There was a sharp whip crack, and then they were gone.

"What's happened?" Sam asked, panic in his voice.

"There was no attempt to damage the bridge," shouted Mason. "We waited all day. No one came."

"But that's impossible!" Meg cried. "Jamie told me that … " Her voice petered out.

A flash of lightning split the sky. Thunder rumbled through the heavens. The rain seemed to pause for a moment, the sky opened, and it began to pour. The rain splashed against the trees and tracks. Dust turned into heavy mud.

"Come on!!" Sam shouted over the rain.

Mason jumped up to the cab. Sam opened the throttle and was shouting for more steam. "We've got to catch them! We can't let them win!!"

Slowly the train rolled across the bridge and began gathering speed. Brit was working in earnest now, hauling wood out of the tender and stuffing it in the firebox.

"More pressure!!" Sam shouted. "We need speed!!" It was four miles from the bridge to the camp. The Ryan stage was well ahead. Could they catch it?

The cold wind howled around them. Rain splattered on the windows of the cab and washed into the tender. The train was going faster and faster. The cars rolled and pitched unsteadily on the uneven track, but still Sam shouted for more steam.

Meg tried to think. What had happened to their plan? Had the Ryan boys forced Jamie to tell them the truth? Maybe they had suspected it was a trap. Or maybe … maybe Jamie had lied to her.

Brit was stuffing cordwood into the firebox as fast as he could. As the door was flung open, the flaming red heat waved back at them. When it slammed shut, the flues sucked in the air, and the blaze roared, consuming the wood in a moment. They could hear the water in the boiler seething violently.

Sam had the throttle open full, but still he was not satisfied. "More steam!!" he shouted. "Pour it on! We've got to have power!!"

The wind whistled, steam escaped from the safety valves, black smoke and ashes poured from the stack. They had to be going fifty miles an hour now.

On the highway, Will rose out of his seat as he cracked his whip. The fresh team was in full gallop. Behind them came the three Ryan brothers on horseback, yelling and shouting at the top of their lungs.

They had to win, Jamie thought. He didn't care about the reward any more. All he could think of was winning that race for the Ryan boys and their stage line.

The rain washed down on them. The horses were slathering wet. Will had pulled his hat down over his forehead, and Jamie's hair and face and clothes were awash.

The road had turned into a nightmare. Big puddles had formed, and the surface had become thick mud. Occasionally the coach skidded on the slippery surface. Clods were being thrown up by the horses and the wheels were spinning liquid mud high in the air. Will urged his horses on, shouting at them, using his whip, slapping the reins across their backs, but the team began to slow.

The steam engine was eating up the miles. Meg could see the road a hundred yards to the east. Occasionally they passed a wagon like it was standing still. No horse could keep up to their pace.

"There it is!!" the girl screamed.

Will Ryan's four-horse stage was galloping along the road as fast as the animals could go in the heavy mud.

Meg could see her brother soaked with rain. Beside him the coachman looked over his shoulder at the approaching train. Again and again he cracked his whip over his horses' heads. But it did no good. The train gained on the stage with every second.

Just as they drew even, Meg pulled the cord of the whistle and gave a long blast of steam. They left the stage behind. A minute later Sam was applying the brakes. They were coming into the construction camp.

"We did it!!" the engineer was shouting. "We beat him, and we did it fair and square." Sam put his arms around Meg and started a wild jig. As they swung out of the cab, a crowd of labourers surged out of the cook tent to greet them.

It was not long before they heard the sound of horses. Will Ryan steered his muddy stagecoach down by the tracks and drew it up beside the locomotive. The animals were completely played out from the hard run. Even though it had stopped raining, Will and Jamie were both soaked and splattered. After he had drawn to a stop, Will waited until an uneasy quiet came over the large crowd.

"So, Sam Bolt, you think you won your race?" the stage driver drawled.

The engineer had his hands deep in the pockets of his overalls. "Looks that way to me."

A slow smile came across Will's face. "I could say it was the rain and the mud, but ... but I guess you won the wager."

The sound of hooves came from out on the road. The crowd of railroaders parted, and the three Ryan brothers on horseback drew up beside the coach. They looked wary.

Sam waited until the crowd had settled before saying, "The day of the horse and stagecoach is over. Railroads are king in this country."

"I've been a horseman all my life, but I guess I have to say that there ain't no way I can compete," Will said.

Mr. Mason stepped forward. "We have a few other things to settle." There was a hard edge to his voice. "I accuse you Ryans of causing damage to the rail line."

Will glanced uneasily at Bobby.

"One of you burned our equipment in a fire and dropped the tree across the track. There were other incidents as well."

"It won't happen no more," said the stage driver.

"Won't happen? How can I believe you?" the superintendent asked.

"I'm a man of my word."

"Jamie Bains knows who caused these problems." Mason looked at the boy sitting on the stage. "You must have enough information to send someone to jail for a long time. If you testify in court against the Ryans, I will give you the two-hundred-dollar reward I promised."

Jamie looked at Bobby nervously sitting on his horse. He glanced at Will. Then his eyes met Meg's.

"Will you do it, boy?" the superintendent demanded.

Jamie swallowed. Meg's eyes were pleading. But, slowly, he shook his head. "I ... I can't. Will says the damage will stop, and I believe him. I ... I guess I'll have to do without the reward. I'm sorry, Meg." His sister was staring at the ground, as still as stone.

"Then there's no money for you."

"But that ain't fair," said Will Ryan. "You said the reward was for anyone who could put an end to all the trouble. This boy done just that. If it weren't for him that bridge would have been nothin' but matchsticks."

"Is that true?"

"I know that for a fact. If you're a man of your word, you owe him two hundred dollars."

"But how do I know there won't be more trouble?"

Will smiled. "The Ryan boys are gettin' out of the stagecoach business. We can't compete against the railway. Maybe we'll take up farmin'."

"Well ... "

"The boy earned her fair and square."

"If you say he saved the bridge, and there will be no more trouble then ... then I guess the money's his."

Jamie couldn't believe his ears. Two hundred dollars. For Mother .... He leapt to the ground from the stage and hugged his sister.

Suddenly Meg hesitated for a moment. "But ... but, Jamie, why did you lie to me about the bridge?"

The boy wasn't sure what to say. "You wouldn't have believed anything else, Meg. And ... and maybe I thought, well, that the Ryans deserved a chance to win the race."

"But ... " Meg shook her head. She was silent for a moment. "I ... I guess you're right, Jamie. I made it hard for you to tell the truth." She smiled at him timidly. Her brother beamed.

"All right, you men," Mason was shouting. "Back to work. We've got a railway to build here!" As the crowd was beginning to break up, he turned to the horsemen. "Why don't you come in to have a cup of Mr. Henry's tea? We've got a lot to talk about."

Will was laughing. "Only if Sam Bolt is buyin'."

"Why not Jamie? He's the one with the big winnin's today."

CHAPTER 18

A S the freight train blew its whistle, announcing that it was ready to leave for the south, Meg went to talk to the engineer. "Do you mind stopping in Exeter?" she asked. "My brother works there, and he needs a ride into London."

"This ain't no passenger train, girl," said the hard-bitten trainman. "Why don't the boy take the stagecoach?"

She tried to argue, but there seemed to be no way that the engineer would relent. When the call of "All aboard" came, Meg grabbed her bags, climbed into the boxcar, and they were off.

Things had been easier for the past few weeks. Meg had worked in the kitchen until the railway was completed. It happened amazingly quickly. Once they got north of Clinton, the country was more rolling. There were a number of rivers and streams to bridge and deep cuts and fills. Despite the problems, the gandy dancers worked at breakneck speed laying almost a mile of track a day. By mid-December, when the snow was starting to fly, they were finished.

Jamie had continued working as the stable boy in Exeter. He liked the job. It was a relaxed, easy pace and there always seemed to be something new to learn about horses.

But the best time in those weeks was when they deposited the two-hundred-dollar reward in the bank at Exeter and sent a cheque home. Jamie had never felt prouder than when he sat down with his sister to pen a letter to the family. Meg's words were glowing.

> It really is Jamie we have to thank for this. I used to think that he was just a little kid, unable to look after himself, but these last few weeks have shown him to be more grown up than I gave him credit for.

It was satisfying to think that after all the trouble between them, they could feel good about each other again.

In November Sam had gone down to London to load up with more construction supplies. When the train had come back, there was a stranger at the controls. Meg asked Mr. Mason what had happened, and he said that Sam had got a new assignment, and he was off working on another line. Still, it seemed strange that he would disappear without saying goodbye.

After the track was finished to Wingham, the company paid off the labourers. The men packed up their gear, and the railroad took them south to London in empty boxcars. Most had a good six months' work from the company. They would be scattering all over North America to look for more work, but at least they had a few dollars in their kit.

Meg was among the last to go. She said goodbye to Mr. Henry. In those last few weeks she had even managed to get along with him a little better, but still she was not sad to see the end of the hard work and the cook's constant nagging.

The train steamed south, passing familiar sights of towns and former camps. On the bridge across the Sable River, she leaned out of the car to look at the deep gully. A mile south, they came into Exeter. Meg hung out the door of the boxcar looking for her brother.

Two horsemen with broad slouch hats waited by the side of the tracks. One was on the back of a sleek, cream-coloured horse, and the other on a big black with a diamond on its forehead. It took her a moment to realize that the pair were Jamie and Will Ryan.

The engineer blew the whistle as the locomotive came abreast of them. The horses reared nervously. The train was not slowing.

"Jamie!!" Meg shouted from the doorway of the boxcar. "Jamie!!"

Her brother took off his hat and waved it at her as the cars rushed by. Then, laughing, he booted his horse and began to race after the speeding train. Faster and faster he galloped, with Will right behind. The two were shouting and laughing, racing their horses with every ounce of strength and skill.

"Come on, Jamie!" Meg was shouting. "You can make it!!"

The horse flew along the ground. Now it was going the same speed as the train. Jamie steered next to the boxcar until he was inches away. With one hand he reached out and grabbed a rung of the ladder. The horse was still in a full gallop when he kicked his feet out of the stirrups and stood up on the saddle. Then he leapt into space and swung onto the train.

"Yip … yahoo!!!" Will yelled as he grabbed the reins of Jamie's horse. He held his hand up in a signal of goodbye while the boy did the same. Their words were lost in the sounds of the engine and the big steel wheels.

Meg marvelled at her brother. He was taller now. His shoulders were broad, and he was heavier. Soon he would be a man.

An hour later the freight train came into the railroad yard in London. Meg and Jamie jumped off, hitched their gear over their shoulders, and hiked back to the station. Meg went into the office to collect her final pay and found Mr. Mason leaning back on a chair, talking to the station-master. She went over with Jamie to say goodbye.

"Too bad you can't go to the big banquet they're having for the railway," the superintendent said, smiling.

"What banquet's that?" Jamie asked.

"They're going to have a splendid affair at London City Hall. All the important people from the communities up and down the line will come in to celebrate the opening of the London, Huron and Bruce Railway. There'll be speeches and toasts to the Queen. It will be a wonderful time."

"Too bad the real people who built the railway can't be there," said Meg with a touch of bitterness.

"What do you mean?"

"The workers. Their sweat built that line."

Mason smiled. "You've got a strange way of seeing things, Meg."

Half an hour later they were out on the wooden platform of the Great Western station when they heard the blast of a steam whistle. A train was arriving from the east.

"The Hamilton passenger express!" the blue-coated stationmaster called. A mob surged to the front of the platform.

Slowly the train came into the station with its bell ringing. Jamie couldn't take his eyes off the magnificent new steam locomotive polished to the point of gleaming. The engineer who drove this train loved his machine.

"Look!!" Meg said excitedly. "It's Sam!"

Sam Bolt, dressed in new denim overalls and bowler hat, was hanging out the window of the cab of his locomotive. He had become an engineer of a passenger express train, the elite of the service, and the gleam on his red face showed how proud he felt.

They were about to run up to the engine to see him, when they heard a call. "Meg!! Jamie!!"

It was their mother with the two younger children, Kate and Rob. They had arrived.

About the author

Bill Freeman was born in London, Ontario, on October 21, 1938. He attended Tecumseh Public School and South Collegiate. After graduating from high school he spent a year in Alberta and three years in London, England. On returning to Canada he attended Acadia University in Nova Scotia, graduating in 1964.

When he had finished university Mr. Freeman moved to Hamilton, Ontario, where he worked for three years as a Probation Officer. After taking an M.A. in Sociology at McMaster University, he worked as a community organizer for a year before he began work as a lecturer at the university. Ph.D. studies followed two years of teaching. He received his doctorate in sociology in 1980. His areas of concentration are labour and political organizations.

In 1976 Bill Freeman moved to Montreal and began teaching at Vanier College. Most recently, in August, 1986, he moved back to Toronto and now lives Ward's Island, working as a full time writer.

He is divorced with four children.

In addition to the books in his historical fiction series, Freeman writes play and adult non-fiction.

In the Same Series

Shantymen of Cache Lake

Winner of the 1976 Canada Council Award for Juvenile Literature, *Shantymen of Cache Lake* is an exciting adventure story that vividly portrays life in Canada of the 1870s.

This is the story of 14-year-old John Bains and his sister Meg, 13, and the winter they spend working in a lumber camp in the Ottawa Valley. The story reaches a dramatic end with the dangerous and exciting log drive down to Quebec City.

The Last Voyage of the Scotian

Meg and John Bains are in Quebec City ready to return to their family when a flashily dressed man tricks them into signing on as a crew on a square-rigged ship.

The windjammer is old, leaky and undermanned and most of the crew have been shanghaied on board. But the dangers are balanced by the excitement for John and Meg of learning the work of sailors.

First Spring on the Grand Banks

John and Meg Bains and their sailor friend Canso come back to Nova Scotia after a transatlantic voyage only to find that Canso's father has died and his schooner has been seized for debts. When they are refused credit for a fishing expedition, they take the schooner and flee to Newfoundland. But the law catches up with Canso and the Bainses in this exciting tale of shipwreck and the Grand Banks fishery.

Trouble at Lachine Mill

The fourth book in Bill Freeman's exciting adventure series is set in Montreal, where Meg Bains and her twelve-year-old brother Jamie take jobs in a shirt factory. They discover that they have been hired at rock-bottom wages to replace striking workers, and the anger of the strikers turns out to be only the beginning of their troubles.

Harbour Thieves

The adventures of Meg and Jamie Bains continue with an exciting story of youngsters living by their wits in the Toronto of 1875. They start out selling newspapers on the street, where they fall in with a lawless gang of street kids and a couple of ne'er-do-well adults. Jamie is forced to join a theft ring and is caught by the police. But he has hunch about where the loot is stashed on Toronto Island: finding it is his one chance to avoid a future in the reformatory.

Teachers' guides are available from the publisher. Write to:
James Lorimer & Company
35 Britain Street
Toronto, Ontario, M5A 1R7